SPARROW

DEFIER SERIES BOOK TWO

MANDY FENDER

Editor: Elizabeth Miller

Book Cover Design: Paper and Sage Design

ISBN-13: 978-0692745915

Stouthearted Publishing

Yea, though I walk
through the valley of
the shadow of death,
I will fear no evil: for
thou art with me; thy
rod and thy staff they
comfort me.

Psalm 23:4

Chapter 1

I can do all things through Christ who strengthens me.

Lennox ran to the crumpled body in front of her. Her new-found friend lay bloodied on the training room floor. Red, sticky goo covered Macey's pale, freckled skin. The fake blood blended in with her vibrant red hair. Lennox knelt beside her unmoving body.

Assess, stabilize, move... assess, stabilize, move....

Tucked away in Sparrow City—under the hills of Texas country—Lennox trained to become a Sparrow medic. A team of recruits who impersonated the enemy approached. Sweat poured from Lennox's hairline. A two-foot high barricade separated her from the encroaching team. Red lasers scanned the room, mimicking the weapons the Regime used.

One of the lead medics—Medic Sanders—spoke instructions into Lennox's ear com. He had positioned himself in the viewing room above the training center so he could watch Lennox's every move.

1

"Assess the damage to the body, stabilize, and move," he coached.

Lennox obeyed. Her nerves weighed heavy with pressure.

"Can you hear me?" Lennox asked, noticing Macey's closed eyes.

No answer. Medics must have told her to act unconscious.

Lennox wished her mother were alive to help her and give all the wisdom gained through years of nursing. She hoped she watched from Heaven. She wanted to make her mother proud.

Lennox checked her patient's head. A faux gash spread from Macey's right eyebrow to her left ear. Red hair mixed with the gash, making it hard to tell exactly how serious the injury was supposed to be. Lennox moved to the next area of her friend's body, pulling the heavy pack off Macey's back and loosening the bullet-resistant armor she wore. Even with armor on, Sparrows could endure fatal injuries. In war, there were no guarantees.

"Assess, stabilize, and move, Lennox. Let's go." Medic Sanders hastened her.

"Yes, sir."

Lennox checked Macey's abdomen. A small hole oozed fake blood at her side. Lennox responded quickly and held gauze to it. The "enemy team" crept closer.

"Stabilize and move. Let's go. No time to waste." Medic Sanders played distracting noises over the training center's intercom. The deafening sounds of gunfire, blasts, and screaming filled the room, recreating the havoc and confusion Sparrows would face in real combat. He had explained that training through distracting noises would help condition the recruits' minds to think during real chaos and authentic crisis.

Come on, Lennox. Move, move, move....

Lennox muted out the pandemonium and hurried to stabilize her friend to the best of her ability. She dragged Macey toward the "safe zone," trying to keep both their bodies protected. Macey did not weigh much, but Lennox still wasn't fast enough. Two "enemies" crouched down behind the barricade she just left. A red laser met her chest and within a millisecond her vest lit up bright blue.

Drill over.

If it had been real she would be dead, and so would Macey. Lennox let out an exasperated breath.

Macey stood up and nudged Lennox with her elbow. "You'll get it next time." She wiped the synthetic blood that dripped in her eyes.

Lennox bit the inside of her cheek as Medic Sanders approached.

"Recruits, line up." Medic Sanders held a tech screen in his hand. He looked at it before addressing the recruits.

They stood in even lines across the room as Medic Sanders paced.

"In the field, there will be times when technology fails and your skills have to step in. That's why we train with and without it. Always be aware of your surroundings. Give good care, but also remember you will be in live combat. The sooner you stabilize and get to a safe zone, the better… for both of you."

"Yes, sir!" the recruits said in unison.

Lesson learned. Keep eyes open. Stay aware of surroundings.

She couldn't let it happen again. Lennox was

determined to succeed. She already defied Ahab, proving her ability to stand and stand alone, if necessary. Now Lennox needed to learn how to fight.

Medic Sanders held the screen behind his back. "Get cleaned up and meet me in the east training classroom. We have a special guest coming in today."

Lennox waited for Macey to clean all the fake blood from her abdomen and face.

"What do you think today's lesson will be?" Macey asked, brushing her hair out of her face with her hands.

"I'm not sure," Lennox answered. Sparrow City provided new lessons every day. Some were harder to learn than others.

Walking into the classroom, Lennox and Macey found chairs next to one another in the front and waited for the lesson to begin.

"As a combat medic, you will see, hear, and smell just how much the body can endure and how far your body can be pushed." Medic Sanders gestured for a Sparrow to stand in front with him.

She had curly brown hair, which was braided to the side. A red medic badge, along with stripes of

5

honor, was sewn onto her gray Sparrow uniform. The petite woman—whom Lennox guessed was in her mid-thirties—did not look big enough to drag grown men to safety, but her honors proved she had.

"This is Medic Holmes. She will be sharing what it's like to be a medic during live combat. Medic Holmes, the class is yours." Medic Sanders took a seat to the side.

Medic Holmes nodded. "Thank you, sir." She addressed the students. "We, as Sparrows, are at an advantage. We can combine our knowledge and training with the wisdom we have from the Word of God. We ought to always be of good courage because God's mercy and His miraculous power are always available to us. Even where our medical methods are insufficient, God is able to heal. And He does. I've seen it over and over again." Though Medic Holmes' tone was gentle, she spoke with authority as one who possessed much hard-earned wisdom. This brave young woman had been where Lennox was going. Lennox leaned forward in anticipation of what she would learn next. She listened intently.

Medic Holmes ran images from her handheld tech

screen onto the large main screen behind her. Moving to the side to give every student a clear view, Holmes narrated the slide show.

"These are the very things you will encounter," she said, as pictures of wounded Sparrows and civilians appeared on the screen.

Lennox wrung her hands together and forced herself to look as images of mangled bodies, bruised and bloodied faces, dislocated arms, broken legs, and bullet-ridden chests flashed before her.

Not women and children. How could they?

Although, it should come as no surprise, Lennox could not believe her own eyes.

As if reading Lennox's mind, Medic Holmes asserted, "You will see women and children injured right along with Sparrow soldiers. The Regime is ruthless. They don't care who you are or how old you are. I have seen these things firsthand with the sounds of bombs in the background and the red lasers of Regime weapons aimed in my direction." She paused to let the recruits absorb her words.

"I am showing you these images so that you will be able to encounter them in real life without surprise, and without hesitation." She pointed to the screen. "*This* is our job. I won't tell you that it will be easy. Often you'll be running on zero sleep when you're called into duty. Many times, you will want to give up... curl into a ball and cry because of the horrors to which you've been exposed. You will want to flee, but you can't. Too many people need you." She looked right into Lennox's eyes as she continued. "With help from God, you will save lives."

She cleared the screen and scanned the entire student body. "You are all here for a reason. As long as you are willing, God will use you in extraordinary ways."

She smiled as she yielded the platform to her host. "Medic Sanders."

Sanders took the stage. "Thank you, Ms. Holmes for a job well done." Addressing the class, Medic Sanders continued, "I know this material was hard to see. Take heart, recruits. You can and *will* make a difference. His deep conviction motivated. "You're dismissed."

Lennox stood from the table and swallowed hard. The images in the slideshow were terrible, but they were exactly why she chose to be a medic. She was determined to bring healing where the Regime caused devastation. God was with her, and through His strength, she would make a difference. She had to. Lives depended on it.

Thirty days into training—her journey from Defier to Sparrow had only just begun.

Chapter 2

Nightmares nagged Lennox's sleep. No... not nightmares... *memories.*

Unable to rest, she threw on a Sparrow sweatshirt and a pair of gray sweatpants to roam the halls. Maybe a glass of cool water would relieve the tension in her nerves. She wanted light... visible light... to dispel the darkness of her night visions. Anything to distract her from their terror. Even in the safety of Sparrow City, she couldn't shake disturbing dreams of the Regime and their demented leader, Ahab. They lurked in her subconscious, beckoning her to give up. But God had done too much for her to quit now.

Lennox stretched and stood to her feet. She arranged the gray wool blankets neatly on her bed. Instructor Easton expected pristine beds when she checked them in the morning.

Lennox looked at her bunkmate—twelve-year-old Clover—who peacefully slept on the top bunk. Not wanting to disturb her, she tiptoed out of the dormitory.

Sparrow scientists equipped all underground corridors with blue lights. They illuminated automatically as Lennox approached and turned off as she passed to conserve energy. The lights always reminded Lennox of the Psalm that talked about God's Word being *a lamp unto her feet and a light unto her path*. When she needed it, the light would be there for her, no matter how dark it got.

After the struggle with Ahab, Lennox learned that quoting Scriptures helped her the most. By doing so, she took authority over the terror that tried to attach itself to her. She took rogue thoughts captive with obedience to Christ and verbally rehearsed the Lord's goodness toward her. Lennox's greatest joy in life came from Scripture, even though she was safe in Sparrow City and surrounded by family and friends. God's Word comforted her in the uttermost depths of her soul. It overcame every tormenting thought and filled her with peace.

God will fulfill His purpose for me. If God be for me, who can be against me?

Lennox saw that God gave her a priceless weapon

in the Scripture, and she employed it often by memorizing and quoting it at every opportunity. Try as they might, nightmares could not wreck her because she had surrendered her whole heart to God.

Lennox continued walking until she reached the double doors that led straight into the large kitchen that was already lit. Entering the room, she was startled to see her best friend, Sky. He sat on a stool and hunched over one of the stainless steel counter tops while drinking an energy drink. He studied what appeared to be a very large hologram map as he wore the same Sparrow sweatshirt as Lennox. He pushed the sleeves to the middle of his forearms, exposing tan skin and tight muscle. As Sky moved red dots around with his pointer finger, he highlighted certain areas of the map.

The thud of the door swinging closed caused Sky to look up. His eyes brightened and a tender smile filled his face when he saw her. Butterflies swirled in her stomach. She often chided herself inwardly for thinking romantically about Sky, given the current state of the world. But Sky was special. He understood what she said even when words failed her, and he made her feel safe and at home no matter where they were. Being around him made her the best version of herself. Lennox wasn't one to throw around a word like "love," but no lesser term could accurately describe the depth of her admiration and respect for him.

As for Sky's feelings about her, Lennox knew he cared for her and certainly valued her as a comrade and fellow soldier, but she was unsure if he felt anything beyond friendship. When Sky pictured his future, did he envision a home and a wife? Maybe even children? And if so, how did she factor in? Much as Lennox longed to broach the subject, she didn't want to make her feelings awkward between them, so she kept true to her "wait-and-see" approach.

Lennox reminded herself that now was not the time for wishful thinking. They both needed to focus on the war and the people God intended them to help. Lennox wanted to fully support Sky and his intention to excel in Sparrow training, but his resolve often frightened her. Losing him was not something she could bear to even contemplate. His friendship meant more to her than she could ever describe.

"Lennox, it's only three a.m. You usually sleep till at least five. Is everything all right?" Sky's concerned voice brought her back to the present.

Heat rushed Lennox's cheeks under his scrutinizing gaze as he abandoned his map and looked directly into her eyes.

"Are you feeling all right?" His tone was tender.

"Just nightmares, again." Lennox smiled, truly comforted by the sight of her friend. His presence made her feel entirely safe, as if nothing and no one could harm her as long as she was under his protection.

Lennox believed God had divinely paired them together so they could support one another through their future struggles. After all, it was Sky who was by Lennox's side when she nearly died from a Regime bomb that devastated their high school prom. The same attack had claimed the life of Kira—the third amiga in their close-knit group. It had been Sky and his grandfather who gave Lennox a home after the death of her parents and the recruitment of her only brother, Oliver, who left to join the Sparrows. Sky was the one who helped Lennox escape a Regime raid. Together, they survived the harrowing journey to Sparrow City. Together, they overcame every obstacle. Lennox would not be where she was without Sky. He was truly a gift from God in her life.

Sky patted a vacant stool beside him. "Here, sit down. I'll get you some water."

He stood up, found a glass, and turned on the faucet.

"I'm okay, Sky, really. I just couldn't fall back to sleep."

Sky set the glass in front of Lennox. "Do you want to talk about it?"

"Not really." Lennox hated reliving the subconscious horrors of the Regime and did her best to not talk about it to anyone, except God. She did not want to burden Sky's heart with her dark memories.

"Well, you're welcome to sit in here with me." He lowered his head and raised his brows. "No talking required if you don't want to." He turned back to his map.

"What are you working on?" Lennox peered over his shoulder to see his project.

The map looked a whole lot like the assignment that they both were expected to submit in a few hours. Lennox had finished hers days ago.

Sky looked sheepish. "It's my map charting

assignment."

"Sky Conners, do you mean to tell me you're *just* finishing the map charting assignment? It is due right after breakfast! And we both know Instructor Easton will not settle for anything less than perfection."

"Not finishing," Sky protested. "Just starting, actually." He chuckled.

Lennox laughed with him, shaking her head. "Procrastinate much?"

Sky came from a long line of disciplined military men. Lennox imagined Sky's ancestors eavesdropping on the conversation from Heaven, rolling their eyes over his antics.

Sky's ability to improvise on the fly was apparent since high school. He regularly put off homework assignments to the last minute, but somehow managed to assemble projects just before time ran out and still get an excellent grade. Lennox hoped his good luck did not run out this time. Sky did not seem at all concerned.

"I'll have you know I do my best work when up against a deadline." He grinned.

"I'll believe it when I see it." Lennox playfully elbowed Sky in the ribs. She smiled at him, pulling her sweatshirt sleeves over her palms. "Do you need any help or am I just in your way?"

"You're never in my way, Lennox. You're my best friend. I do my best work when you're at my side." Sky gently brushed his hand over hers. "I'm not only going to finish this assignment, I am going to ace it. You'll see."

Sky retrieved his hologram map and pulled his stool close enough to sit shoulder-to-shoulder with her. He tapped an adaptor blade on the table and it changed its molecular structure to a geometric compass. The technology the Sparrows created never ceased to amaze Lennox. Sky held the compass onto a paper tablet he had on the table and marked the coordinates for his assignment, one after the other.

Several hours passed and the morning commotion began. Laughter and footfalls filled the hallway outside the kitchen. Sky finished his work and shut down the hologram, putting the assignment in his cargo-pant pocket along with the adaptor blade.

"We better move out of the way for breakfast." He stood and gathered his belongings. "I'm going to get ready for training. I'll meet you there?" He smiled and tilted his head.

Lennox stood and nodded. "Meet you there."

Chapter 3

Jagged earth made up the walls of the combat training room. Blue light emitted from steel bowl shaped fixtures. Black sparring mats, weapons, and Sparrow technology equipped the spacious, underground room. A large cannon-like weapon sat on one of the steel tables. Lennox had yet to be trained for the advanced piece of technology.

Butterflies lifted in her stomach. She could hardly wait. Everything in Sparrow City piqued her interest. Faux debris and barricades were everywhere, positioned so that the Sparrows would learn to use everything to their advantage.

Sparrow recruits from every race, background, and age stood in lines across the room. Sky stood with them. Lennox hastened to his side.

Instructor Easton entered the room and made her way over to the group. She began teaching immediately.

"Recruits, I hope you took your charting assignments seriously. Out in the field, you will need that skill set."

Lennox caught Sky's glance and smirked. He winked at her and smiled back.

Instructor Easton's steps carved a path before the line of new recruits. "In combat, you can't doubt yourself or your skills, and you especially cannot doubt God. You must be physically, mentally, and spiritually ready for whatever comes your way. We don't fight like one beating the air. We know our real weapons are not carnal, but mighty through God."

Lennox reflected on the enormity of the task before her. She had not stood in defiance to walk toward failure now. She would train hard. She would shoulder the pressure. Pressure turned coal into diamonds. Pressure would make Lennox great. She gulped. *Hopefully.*

Lennox remembered back to her first day of training and thought about how far she had come. Back then, she had not even known how to punch properly. Now, she utilized every part of her body as an offensive weapon. She had been taught how to defend herself, even against adversaries far bigger and stronger. Even the gun she practiced with became a part of her—an extension of her very being.

But physical warfare was not the only skill Lennox had sharpened. She had developed the ability to pray and trust God. Lennox prayed hard and often, knowing it would make a difference in war when nothing else could.

"Lennox you're up." Easton pointed to the moving hologram targets.

Lennox snapped to attention and took a deep breath as she stepped onto the center mat. She lifted her weapon—the one the Sparrows referred to as the Blue Striker—because those who were hit by its serum were struck down where they stood. The gun's ammunition was Sparrow regulation grade—glowing blue bullets that held a potent, crippling serum that was enough to bring down even the strongest of men. The serum was not lethal, but the pain it caused made those injected with it wish it were... or so the holograms indicated.

The first time Lennox picked up a Blue Striker, it reminded her of the toy guns utilized in an arcade. It took only one shot for Lennox to realize that video game guns and the weapon in her hand were similar only in shape. The Striker left behind a sting her hands would never forget. It made her realize the true power of what she held. Becoming proficient with the weapon was not a simple task. Lennox still felt she had a lot to learn.

She tucked a loose strand of hair behind her ear—the rest was pulled back into a tight bun. The gray sleeves of Lennox's gray Sparrow uniform were rolled up, exposing the remnants of an injury she'd received when in one of the Regime's prison camps—a silver *D* on the inside of her forearm.

To Lennox, the scar served as a daily reminder of why she should fight. The very sight of it made her push herself farther, run faster, be stronger, and train harder.

Lennox took aim and fired. She missed.

Calm down, take a breath, you got this.

She took aim and fired again, hitting a hologram target.

Phew!

She could only imagine how it would be to open fire on a real, living, breathing person.

"Good." Easton encouraged Lennox. "Don't hesitate to pull the trigger. All it takes is a split second to lose your advantage and be at serious risk."

The scar on Instructor Easton's face reflected a glow from the blue lights that hung above her. Maybe that was how she got her scar—hesitation to pull the trigger.

Lennox nodded and maintained focus as she advanced through the course. Hologram bullets sped toward her face as she maneuvered her body through barrier after barrier. It did not matter that her adversaries were mere holograms. Lennox did not want their shots to even graze her skin. Weeks of training had resulted in Lennox's body contorting in ways she would not have guessed she was capable of.

Armed with the Striker and a Sapphire Shield, Lennox twisted and angled her body under rails and over faux debris. Whenever the enemy shot, she raised her shield and bullets vanished into thin air. The Sapphire Shield was Lennox's favorite tool of defense. It had saved her repeatedly throughout numerous training exercises.

As Lennox labored, Instructor Easton educated the

recruits.

"Once the blue serum enters the enemies' bloodstream, our enemies will be subdued for containment. Many of those we have overcome have begged for death because of the serum's sting, but none will find it." Instructor Easton's voice conveyed her conviction. "God is a good God and, accordingly, everyone is to be given the chance to turn from their evil ways and repent. That is why we don't kill anyone when we have the ability to immobilize. Killing is to be viewed as a grievous necessity of war and as an absolute last resort."

Lennox finished the rest of the course and rejoined the group. Letting out a heavy breath, she bit her bottom lip. The energy exerted made her body sore, but it satisfied her soul. She had displayed both strength and savvy. Maybe Lennox had more natural ability than she gave herself credit.

"Nice work, Lennox." Easton gave an approving glance.

"Thanks." Lennox was pleased with her teacher's praise.

Instructor Easton, though only eight years her

senior at twenty-six, was the best trainer Lennox had encountered. There was something about the way she taught. Her powers of observation were unsurpassed. Her ability to recognize potential threats, problem solve quickly, think, and communicate efficiently in a combat setting would undoubtedly save many soldiers' lives.

Lennox's brother, Oliver, always spoke highly of Instructor Easton and the respect appeared to be mutual. They both became Sparrow Instructors at a young age, and the amount of pressure on their shoulders must be unreal. Though Lennox had yet to detect any romantic affection between the two, she thought they would make a nice couple. Lennox briefly allowed herself to imagine a world where Instructor Easton could spend her morning on a date with Oliver in a coffee shop, instead of in a bunker trying to survive a siege by the Regime. How different life had become.

After turning the safety on her gun, Lennox placed it on a nearby table and rejoined her classmates. She stood by Macey, who squeezed Lennox's hand affectionately.

"Good job!" Macey stood to Lennox's left. She

whispered, "You're going to have to help me."

Lennox smiled at Macey. "I will help you with whatever you need."

They had to stick together if any of them were to succeed. Lennox maintained her high school motto "one for all and all for one." They were all in it together, even if they didn't want to be.

Sky brushed a light hand over Lennox's back, causing her to turn toward him. He raised his right eyebrow and whispered, "You're getting better."

"Thanks, still not as good as you." Lennox's lips curved into a smile at the sight of his dimples.

Sky had been lean ever since Lennox first met him in kindergarten. Running track had taught Sky endurance and playing baseball and basketball throughout school gave him strong legs and excellent upper body strength. But it was the intense Sparrow workout regimens that added twelve pounds of pure muscle mass to his already athletic frame. From the beginning of training, Sky impressed with physical prowess and intelligence. His adaptability caught the attention of all the trainers.

Instructor Easton characterized Sky as a natural

born soldier. Perhaps it was because of his great leadership potential that she held him to extremely high standards. Lennox knew Sky well enough to understand when he was annoyed, and he had been annoyed by Instructor Easton's constant coaching more than once. Lennox anticipated this time would be no different.

As Sky selected his weapon and approached the course, Instructor Easton paced.

"Listen recruits, no matter who you are, there's always room for improvement."

The new soldiers groaned under their breath. It was the thousandth time they heard this from her this week, but she was right. No matter how great the previous attempt had been, she expected the next result to be better—vastly better.

Chin high and shoulders squared, Sky walked to the starting position, his green eyes were focused… determined.

The tech coordinators released a legion of hologram soldiers and the simulation began. Sky fired his weapon, taking out three holograms. Seven more took their place.

Seven?

Lennox re-counted. Most recruits were only required to take on one or two... maybe three... holograms at a time. Seven was unheard of.

Whispers moved up and down the line of recruits. They noticed, too. Lennox watched with intrigue to see what Sky would do next.

He followed two hologram soldiers that appeared to be the biggest threats and took cover behind a concrete barrier. Lennox held her breath as a third hologram appeared behind him. Sky must have sensed it because he turned and pulled the trigger.

Hit!

The fourth, fifth, and sixth holograms crept out, surrounding Sky on all sides. He raised his weapon and fired again, hitting two, but missing one. A high-pitched alarm pierced the air.

Sky had been hit.

Frowning, Sky shook his head and stepped off the mat. He was immediately intercepted by Instructor Easton.

"You have to stop taking on more than is prudent. You did the same thing last drill. Sacrificing yourself when it is not necessary is not noble. It's stupid. Having a Savior Complex doesn't make you a hero. It makes you a liability."

Lennox could not deny that "Savior Complex" accurately described Sky in combat. He always wanted to rescue everyone else. It made sense. It was just Sky being Sky. Lennox sympathized with her friend. No one enjoyed getting called out, especially for doing what they felt was right. Being a protector was a part of his nature. It always had been.

Lennox flashed back to kindergarten when Sky shoved a little boy for teasing her. She suppressed a smile as she remembered his five-year-old face when he was marched to the principal's office. It mirrored his current expression.

Instructor Easton used the situation as a teaching moment and chose to ignore Sky's scowl. She addressed the recruits.

"It is important you remember, you are not in this alone. A one-man army can only do so much. Understand?" She locked eyes with Sky.

Sky nodded and wiped the sweat from his brow with his forearm. "Yes, ma'am."

Lennox patted Sky's arm once he took his place by her side. She wanted to soothe away any embarrassment that Sky may have felt.

"You did really well," she consoled. She hoped he knew that he did not have to be a lone ranger. She wanted to protect him, too—even if it meant protecting him from himself.

"Thanks." Sky smiled slightly, his dimples barely showing on his cheeks. "I have to be reminded not to get cocky, I guess."

A rush of warmth tingled around her heart. What a relief to know Sky recognized one of his few weaknesses. Multiple Sparrow instructors taught that pride could—and would—destroy even the greatest man.

Lennox comprehended Sky had a fire in his belly. She understood that he longed to be the man his grandfather had raised him to be—a man of humility, honor, and respect. But Lennox also understood that tests and making examples of recruits was common among the Sparrow trainers. A recruit's prospect and ability to prove one's self worthy to rise in the Sparrow's ranks directly correlated to their willingness to be teachable. In the estimation of Instructor Easton and that of her counterparts, the more a recruit thought he knew, the more he had to learn.

The training process was definitely a marathon, not a sprint. Lennox would have to help Sky be patient with the process.

The rest of the recruits were put through their paces. Some excelled while others struggled to maintain a good pace on the course. Macey often fell behind. She panted at the end. Lennox patted her shoulder to help lift her spirit. Macey simply nodded in reply.

"Okay, recruits! That's enough for today. We will continue drills in hand-to-hand combat tomorrow. I expect you to come ready with the knowledge you have accrued from the past several weeks. Soon you will be in the field, facing the Regime head on, not as recruits, but as Sparrows. Stay prayed up!"

"Yes ma'am!" the recruits said in unison.

"You are dismissed to your other duties. Lennox and Sky, can you stay with me please?" Easton relaxed as everyone filed out of the training room and headed to their designated assignments. She folded her hands together behind her back.

"It's about the locket, isn't it?" Lennox asked, too eager to wait for Easton to start the conversation. Lennox had been kept in the dark concerning the whereabouts of her mother's locket—the one that could change everything—the one that her father hid the microchip within that could bring the Regime to its knees. She had been dreaming about recovering it and finding out what it could do. She knew Easton had to have news about it. No one was ever called to stay behind after drills.

"There have been several attempts by some of our best to retrieve it. They have not had any luck yet. Right now, a team is in place and we are optimistic that we can access the locket and bring it back to Sparrow City. General Eli has given me permission to keep you updated. He knows you have probably been wondering about it."

Eli was right. She *always* wondered about it. What it could do. What it *would* do. Her father must have created it to stop the Global Weather Simulator and allow the Sparrows the upper hand.

Lennox hated the thought that the Regime had her

mother's locket. Ahab was a merciless dictator and his minions were brutes. The Regime was just like the devil. They came to kill, steal, and destroy. Lennox was tired of the world being in chaos. The GWS held no blows back. If it could change the weather to destroy every last Defier, it would, and it was getting close to doing that. There was no other option for the innocent. The Sparrows had to overthrow the Regime... and soon.

Chapter 4

Lennox walked with Sky into the hallway where Macey waited for them. Macey twisted her hands together over her chest as she rocked back and forth.

"Hey Macey," Sky said.

"Hey," she whispered back, still twisting her hands like a child.

"What's wrong?" Lennox rushed to her side. Her friend didn't wring her hands unless she was nervous.

"Do you think you guys can help me get better at my marksmanship?" Macey swallowed hard. She wasn't the worst shooter, but she wasn't the best either. Her course time could benefit from improved accuracy. Handling a high-powered weapon at her size was probably more difficult. Though with more training, she could do it. Lives depended on that skill.

"Of course." Sky popped his knuckles. "I need the extra practice too. There's always room for improvement." Sky laughed as he repeated Easton's words. "But seriously, I need it too and will help you as much as I can."

"I'll ask Instructor Easton for permission to use the outdoor range." Lennox turned back to the training room. Sky and Macey stayed in the hall.

Instructor Easton conversed with other high ranking Sparrow officers. Lennox wasn't sure how to avoid being rude. As she got closer, she cleared her throat.

"Instructor Easton? Sorry to interrupt, ma'am." She did not know exactly what she interrupted. It looked like casual conversation, but she was sure it wasn't.

"Not a problem, what's wrong?" Easton turned slowly to face Lennox.

"Nothing ma'am. I just wanted to get permission to take Macey to the outdoor range."

"Straight there and straight back. The Regime is camped outside the dome and has been since you arrived, looking for ways to infiltrate Sparrow City. So, stay toward the center while above ground."

"Yes, ma'am."

Lennox heard the stories of the Regime soldiers trying to break through the Sparrow tech, reminding Lennox the realness of the threat beyond the dome.

She walked back to where Macey and Sky waited in the hall. "All right, let's do it."

They strolled to the red metal door that led outside. Sky pressed his hand against the scanner and waited while a thin red line ran up and down his fingertips to his palm, allowing the door to open to a path that led to the outside range.

Gazing at the rolling hills that surrounded them, Lennox closed her eyes and took a deep breath. Oh! How she missed the smell of the tall grass and the fresh earth. Opening her eyes, she peered beyond the Sparrow tech dome. Rippling clouds moved eastward. They were dark and heavy, as if an angry storm could break out above Sparrow City at any moment. She inhaled again, praising God for inspiring the technology that kept them safe. Without it, Sparrow City would have been destroyed long ago.

The three reached the range by walking several yards. Instructors had mounted a command box that controlled the range onto a steel pole. Sky opened the lid and pressed a button. Holograms emerged from the ground before them. Some were far, some up close.

Lennox and Macey headed toward the nearby

weapon dispensary that housed an assortment of weapons. The dispensary lit up as they approached. They placed their hands on the scanner, in turn, and made their selections—the Blue Striker, first, and then a specialized Sparrow handgun. Sky allowed the scanner to read his prints and chose a sniper rifle. No surprise. He had plenty of experience with that style of weapon since Pop often let him shoot a similar rifle back on the farm.

"Okay, Macey," Sky said. "You first."

Lennox walked with her to get in position. The orange holograms raised weapons and moved. Macey lined up the Striker with her mark and pulled the trigger. She missed by a few inches and let out a heavy sigh.

"It's okay." Lennox gave Macey an encouraging smile.

Firing a weapon with little experience was a challenge. Lennox thought back to the first time she fired a gun. The kickback alone bruised her shoulder, which made her appreciate the power behind the weapons she used. "Stay calm, focused, and know you can do this." Lennox continued to encourage as she

37

thought Instructor Easton would.

"Right." Macey nodded. "I can do this." Macey fired again, this time hitting the target, but just barely.

"Better." Sky stood off to the side, looking at where Macey hit. "Now, try it again, but when you line up, inhale, then release the breath as you pull the trigger."

Lennox tossed him a smile, remembering when he gave her the same advice.

Macey lined up her weapon, inhaled, and fired. She hit the target dead center and it disintegrated.

"It worked!" She smiled. "Thank you. I *can* do this." She paused. "I'm going to be able to do this, right?" Her grin faded to a more serious expression. She bit her bottom lip. "I have to."

Lennox and Sky nodded. Macey's simple statement expressed the truth they all shared. The war was real, and they—teenage soldiers, barely old enough to vote—would fight in it. Not that there were going to be elections anymore.

Lennox hugged Macey from the side. "We all have to. It's not going to be easy. We will stick together."

The grittiness of war shaped girls into women and

boys into men. War separated the weak from the strong, the cowardly from the courageous. They all had to be tough, both physically and mentally.

"Your turn." Macey lowered her weapon and moved so Lennox could shoot. Lennox carefully aimed at one of the middle targets, released her breath and pulled the trigger. The hologram stalled in position for a few seconds then continued to move. It wasn't a clean shot. Lennox took aim again and fired. A fantastic display of disappearing orange represented her shot.

"Nice shots, now let's try something a little different," Sky said before he lay on the ground, stomach down in sniper position. "Sometimes the best advantage is distance. If you can learn to shoot at this distance, it will be less dangerous and you'll have the advantage." Sky peered over his shoulder to look at Macey and Lennox. "I'll shoot first to show you how, then you two can take turns on it, okay?"

Lennox and Macey nodded and watched as Sky meticulously lined the sniper rifle in place, released his breath and fired. Hit! He got off the ground and dusted himself off. "Macey, you want to go first?"

"Sure." Macey lay on her stomach and looked

through the scope.

"Take your time." Lennox studied Macey's position in preparation for her turn and waited in silence to allow Macey to concentrate. Macey took several breaths before firing off the first shot.

Sky grabbed the binoculars from the dispensary and held them up. "Are you kidding me?" He held the binoculars down then up to his eyes again. "Macey! That was a direct hit. You obliterated that hologram." He laughed.

Macey's mouth fell open, and she peered through the scope again. "No way."

Sky held out the binoculars for Lennox. She put them to her eyes and saw the last of the orange particles vanish. "Looks like you found your strength."

Macey jumped up and hugged her helpful best friends. "Thanks, guys. This is exactly what I needed."

"We're happy to help." Lennox squeezed Macey's shoulder.

"And we know, no matter who you are..." Sky coaxed the girls to chime in with him. "There's always room for improvement."

The three laughed and, for a minute, the enormous

weight around Lennox's heart lifted and she enjoyed being with her friends. They took turns hitting their marks over the next few hours. Sky encouraged the two and fired off a few rounds himself. Lennox and Macey challenged each other, which built confidence and bravery. If they were going to survive, they needed every ounce of courage confidence brought.

Lennox returned to the Sparrow entrance with Sky and Macey. Inside, Sparrows cried, held hands, and hugged one another with their eyes fixed on tech screens. Lennox stopped in her tracks when she saw the unimaginable. Sky and Macey paused with her and watched in horror, their mouths agape.

Images of the Regime popped up on the live feed screens that lined the halls. Regime soldiers rummaged through the remains of a burning city. They lowered an American flag, ripped it at its seams and spit on the red, white, and blue colors. Then they threw the flag to the ground and set it ablaze. The fire consumed it within minutes.

The destruction sent chills down Lennox's spine and the hair on her arms prickled upward as if a bolt of electricity coursed through her. She couldn't believe her eyes. A few Sparrows shouted in protest. Others grumbled under their breath. Most watched in silence. A few sets of eyes glazed over with obvious numbness. If the Regime took full control, no one would be left free. Gazing at the burning flags upon the screen, Lennox saw the man she despised the most.

Ahab.

He wore his usual attire—a suit with perfectly pressed pants—yet he looked undone… frazzled. With him stood a family, but not just any family. A *defiant* family. They were easily identified by the large, blistering *Ds* that were burned into the flesh of their left forearms. Lennox's fingers involuntary went to her identical wound. Though healed, it forever left a scar on her arm and heart.

The four-member family consisted of a father, a mother, and two small children. Ahab addressed the family, but aimed his gaze directly into the camera. He knew they broadcasted live.

"Deny Christ and live. Refuse… and die."

His cold, calculating words sliced through Lennox's heart. She felt fingers as sharp as knives wrap themselves around her lungs, attempting to squeeze the life out of her. She stood frozen with terror, afraid of what would happen but unable to look away.

The family's patriarch spoke for them all. "As for me and my house, we will serve the Lord." The father's chin rose in defiance and the children cried as they huddled closer to both of their parents.

Ahab forced the family to stand on the burning flag. Lennox coiled her fists, digging her nails into her palms. "No," she murmured. Bile rose in the back of her throat. She broke into a sweat and trembled. The scene reminded her too much of one she witnessed only months before—when her own parents were captured.

One gun-shot fired. Lennox jumped at the sound. A thousand needles pricked against her skin.

The second shot.

No!

Three… four….

It was too much. Her heart couldn't take it.

Sky stepped forward and reached for Lennox's

trembling hand. He held on tight, silently being the rock she needed. She looked up at him and shook her head in disbelief. Lennox buried her head in Sky's shoulder to avoid seeing any more. Loss never got easier, no matter how many times she witnessed it.

The American flag represented good men—Sparrows... *families*... who gave their lives. Now, in its place, a black flag lurched up from the ashes of a torn down city... a torn down family. America, the beautiful, became something else altogether. It was a place unrecognizable. It was no longer the land of the free. It might never be that again. Maybe it could still be the home of the brave, as long as the Sparrows were around.

Easton walked into the tunneled hall behind Lennox and patted her on the back, causing her to look up from the concrete floor. The steel-gray Sparrow uniform skimmed her scars—the scars that Ander inflicted because of her sedition. Lennox comprehended revenge as wrong—that vengeance was the Lord's, but she couldn't help but think of returning on Ander—the person who betrayed her—the same pain he made her feel, returning the same to Ahab.

Ahab deserved the wrath of a million armies against him. Why did evil men get to live, while innocent families didn't?

Lennox let out a release of oxygen through pursed lips. God had a plan for them all. She needed to trust His plan and timing.

Easton tightened her jaw as she walked past the recruits that stared at the screens. Lennox wondered how Easton felt when she saw such atrocities. How much more had she seen? How did she cope? The only way was compartmentalizing. Lennox wasn't so sure she could do that.

Sky kept a firm hold of Lennox's hand as she tried not to cry. God would bring justice. She didn't know how He would turn it all around in their favor, but He never failed. He would come through as He always had.

Lennox closed her eyes and let the tears roll down her cheeks, mourning the loss and grieving her own loved ones.

Lord, I trust you.

The Regime had stolen, pillaged, and killed enough. They had to go down. God would show the

Sparrows how. God would show Lennox how.

Chapter 5

Lennox anticipated an uplifting training session after a hard day before. Every Tuesday the Sparrow recruits had CTT—Critical Thinking Tactics. It was a class that Instructor Easton and fellow team leaders designed to build trusting relationships. It also helped build morale and sharp minds by encouraging healthy competitions. The bonds built during CTT proved to be the best on the field.

A line of recruits walked past the underground training facility and into a spacious virtual simulation room, where each recruit could create their own mission and set up obstacles for the opposing team.

Lennox loved Tuesdays. She stood in a row with her regular team—Macey, Sky, and Sky's bunkmate, Ace. Ace was an MMA fighter before joining the Sparrows. Everyone called him Ace because he always won. He had strong shoulders and onyx skin that made him look like a perfectly chiseled arena warrior with a distinct southern accent. Sky befriended Ace on the very first day of training. They had a lot in common. Ace—the one who never lost, and Sky—the perfect shot, got along just fine as long as they were on the same team. Sky was all heart while Ace relied on logic and that turned out to be quite the advantage in the virtual challenges. For now, they were the rookie team to beat.

Colonel Eldridge crossed his arms, looking at the recruits. He had a thick covering of salt-and-pepper hair on his scalp, black-rimmed glasses, and a lot of stars on his uniform. Stars represented victories, courageous acts, and battle wounds. He was an original Sparrow and an Army veteran before that. He was too old to fight in the field now, but not too old to kick some tail in the virtual training room.

"Why don't we change it up a bit?"

Easton smiled. "Yes, sir." She weaved herself between the recruits. "Alright Sparrows, listen up, this will be a timed challenge. The team with the most left standing wins. Females against males." Easton folded her hands behind her back. "I will head up the women's team. Instructor Oliver Winters will lead the men's.

May the best team win!"

"Oh, we will." Oliver's scruffy battle-time beard was gone. His freshly shaved face revealed smooth, tanned skin as he displayed a grin in Easton's direction.

Easton smirked. She turned on her heel to gather her ten member female army while Oliver moved to his team. Ace and Sky already gave each other a loud pep talk on how they would obliterate the girls—all in team building fun, of course.

Lennox shook her head and whispered to Macey, "Now would be the perfect time for you to have target practice, and *Ace* is your target. Let's bring him down a peg or two."

Macey beamed and gave Lennox a wink. "You got it! Oh, it's on. He doesn't stand a chance. I'm fired up!" She jumped up and down like a boxer preparing to enter the ring. Lennox loved her enthusiasm.

Colonel Eldridge explained the rules in better detail. "Each team will have fifteen minutes to set up their virtual defenses, as well as offenses. Choose your zones wisely and remember your mission is to infiltrate the opponent's course without getting caught. The team with the most standing on the other side at the end of the hour, wins. The reward will be no cleaning duties for the day. The losing team will pick those extra duties up. The fifteen minutes start… now!"

Recruits bustled and shoved their way to their zones.

After creating their world, Easton motioned for the female recruits to follow her to the wall of computers on the north side of the virtual room. "Okay, ladies, the men have the advantage only in hand-to-hand combat because of strength. We have the upper hand on discipline. As long as we keep them at a distance, we'll maintain our advantage. What is the best course of action to do this?" Easton never missed an opportunity to teach the recruits how to think on their feet.

"Our defenses need to be strong," Lennox said.

"Right. And our offense?"

"We set a team to cover those who advance," Macey added.

"Precisely." Easton typed in commands on the computer, the screen displayed the virtual course as if it were a real world. "Here are your helmets. As soon as you put them on they will be live. The men, no doubt, have set up counter-maneuvers. That's when you have to think, weigh your options, and act."

Easton handed a black helmet with a darkened visor and a headset to Lennox, along with a gun that lit up if one player shot another. "You, Cat, Julia, and Ashton are our defense. Defend our area while the rest of us advance. You got that?"

"Yes, ma'am." Lennox took the helmet and put it on. Immediately the world they created spread before her. Easton chose a wrecked building with twisted metal and broken cement for cover. Virtual snow and ice covered the outside of the building. Breath fogged from her mouth as a shiver wobbled her spine. A realistic virtual experience, as always.

"Fifteen minutes are up! You are live!" Colonel Eldridge placed a helmet on his head, entering into the recruits' worlds.

Lennox spoke into the headset. "Cat, cover east. Julia, west. Ashton, cover back territory. I will take forward center."

"Got it," the three responded, getting to their positions.

The men wasted no time firing. Flashes of blue light whizzed by Lennox's head. She ducked down behind a fallen piece of virtual building. Snow fell from above. Lennox peaked over the barricade at the men's world.

The men's world was dark—a forest of tall trees and rocks. Smart. They constructed a realm where their strength could shine. The two worlds met in the center where a line of snow, metal, and cement met the realm of dark green and silver moonlight.

"Cat, Julia. Can y'all cover me?" Lennox had to get to the center if her team ever stood a chance of making it to their mark.

"We got you. Go!" Cat said.

Cat and Julia fired their weapons toward the trees. Flashes of blue and red collided. Lennox army-crawled to a virtual cement barricade and took cover, positioning herself at just the right angle. Close to the center, two male recruits hid behind a boulder. She realized they did not see her coming because they stuck their heads out too far. She fired and the one on the right lit up bright blue.

Yes!

"Nice shot." Easton whispered through the headset.

The other recruit stayed tucked behind the boulder. Lennox looked ahead. Easton had already made her way past the line, two yards from where Lennox had just fired her shot.

"I got him on my side." Julia fired her weapon. The stone shone blue. She barely missed. The recruit scrunched behind the boulder further. Julia changed the angle of her weapon. She fired again. This time, he lit up blue. "Oh, YEAH!" she shouted.

Two down.

"Easton, how y'all doing up there?" Lennox asked.

"We've lost three. There's not much cover over here. We need an active shooter keeping an eye on us. Move up."

"Yes ma'am." Lennox started to make her way forward. "Ladies, you hear that?"

"We got you. Go. I will stay back here," Ashton said.

Lennox moved up as ordered. She was now parallel with one of her opponents. Adrenaline pushed through her veins as her heart thudded. He saw her.

One... two... three shots landed beside her, giving away her position to the rest of her rivals. Her cement barricade lit up like a Christmas tree. She hit the ground and rolled toward the line. She took refuge behind a wide tree trunk. It reminded her of the tree she once hid behind to evade a Regime soldier. She refocused. As she released her breath, she turned to fire, but one of her teammates already took the shot, successfully lighting him up. He held his weapon in the air and exited the course.

Three down.

A timer scrolled across her visor screen—twenty minutes left. Time flew by. It felt like only a few minutes had passed, not forty. How close were the others? How many still stood?

"Update," Lennox requested.

"We lost one more. Six of us left. How many have you girls taken out?" Easton asked.

"Three, so far."

"Make that four." Macey came in for the first time since they began.

"Macey? You got one?" Easton sounded proud and a little surprised.

"Not just anyone. *The* one. I got Ace!" Macey let out a squeal of delight through the com. She'd been working hard. It was about time it showed on the course.

"You're going to have to tell me about that one," Lennox said. Ace would never live it down. Macey would remind him if he did. Lennox and Sky would too.

"Great job, Mace!" Easton said.

"Way to go, Macey!" the other girls chimed in.

Ace held his weapon in the air and left the course, shaking his head as he joined the others, defeated.

Ten minutes.

"Lennox, are you on the men's course?" Easton asked.

"Yes, ma'am." Lennox studied her surroundings. They were dark, wooded, and cold.

"Can you make it to the mark?" Easton questioned.

Lennox observed Easton's position—she was close to twenty yards away from the mark.

"I think so." Lennox would have to hustle.

Nine minutes.

"Do it." Easton made the call, and Lennox obeyed.

She crept to one tree, and then the other. No shots fired. Then she met Oliver, face-to-face. He held up his gun and Lennox froze.

"You wouldn't," Lennox said, trying to distract him. He hesitated for a split second, which was all it took. His body turned bright blue through the visor.

Easton stood behind him with her finger still on the trigger. "You hesitated." She shook her head.

Never hesitate. Lesson learned.

Oliver bit his bottom lip and tilted his head. "Oh, I see how it is." He lifted his gun in the air and walked off the course.

Two minutes.

"Get to the mark!" Easton rushed to the boulder that represented the infiltration point. Lennox hustled behind her.

Simulation over.

Colonel Eldridge stepped out onto the center of the course. "You may remove your helmets. All team members, please gather in the center."

The vivid realms vanished and were replaced by gray walls and floors.

"Both teams fought a valiant fight. But this round goes to…" Colonel Eldridge paused to add suspense. "The female recruits!" He smiled. "Congratulations recruits. Your cleaning duties belong to the men today. Keep up the good work. Men, better luck next time."

With that, Colonel Eldridge walked to his office, shutting the door behind him. He would review the footage recorded from the helmets and give each recruit a review of their performance. He would also post the outcome on the live feed as an additional reward to show the highlights of the day and provide the more valuable prize—bragging rights.

Oliver pressed his lips together, shaking his head. "I can't believe you shot me in the back, Easton."

"You were the one who hesitated." Easton patted Oliver on the back and smiled, her scar curved as she did.

"I see how it is. I'm glad we are on the same side then." Oliver joked.

Lennox's mind was relieved to see the weight of the world off his shoulders for once. Most days he maintained a serious demeanor, which was expected with all he saw outside Sparrow City.

Sky congratulated Macey and Lennox. Ace congratulated them, his square jaw tightened and his chiseled face pressed harder together into an unpleased scowl. Lennox could tell he knew the jokes were coming.

"Ace, what happened to you out there?" Sky questioned.

"I heard Macey got you." Lennox leaned toward Macey and gave her a high-five. "Looks like the extra training paid off."

"It certainly did. Ace had a good run...but..." Macey laughed.

"Yeah, yeah. I don't want to talk about it." Ace rolled his dark eyes as he let out a hard, heavy breath.

"Aw, too soon?" Lennox teased.

"I guess you don't win them all. Maybe we should call you Ace only some of the time now," Macey joked. She needed the extra boost in confidence and Ace needed the lesson in humility. It was a win-win scenario.

"All of you, good job." Oliver high-fived the group. "But next time is ours."

"Good luck with that." Easton smiled.

The six continued to banter until the room fell quiet. Easton held a hand to her right ear, the same ear she kept a com in.

"Oliver, we have to go." Her smile turned flat as she spoke seriously. "Good round, guys. We'll see you all later."

"Y'all get some rest. We'll talk soon." Oliver walked behind her in haste.

Chapter 6

Sirens rang while red lights flashed inside the blue-lit tunnels of Sparrow City. At this hour, the tunnels were usually empty and quiet. Now, the lights and sirens stirred the halls with loud commotion. A rush of people in gray moved throughout the tunnels. Some Sparrows hurried in, others out. Hard soles clunked against the cement floor, not in marching rhythm but in scattered panic.

Lennox stood at the far end of the hallway, Sky and Oliver on either side of her, as the chaos ebbed closer. Easton ran toward them. Her beautiful face was pressed into a hard scowl. "Come with me. Quickly!"

They followed her immediately to the entrance of a trauma ward.

"They were just brought in, barely got them past the Regime." Easton directed Sparrows to the infirmary located to the right. It was closest to the entrance of the tunnels and hidden behind the holograms of cherry blossom trees.

"What happened?" Oliver asked one of the uninjured Sparrows.

"We were out scouting when the weather grew fierce from the Global Weather Simulator. And then... out of nowhere... Regime soldiers had us surrounded. They bombarded us with heavy artillery."

Another Sparrow—who had a bandage over his eye—chimed in. "We passed a blockade and within seconds, we were ambushed. I don't think they are taking prisoners anymore. They're shooting to kill."

It seemed like the Regime had the upper hand because Sparrows surely didn't. One after another, the injured were carried into the ward. Mangled limbs, blood, and distraught faces filled Lennox's view.

"Lennox, start over there," Easton shouted while pointing to soldiers on gurneys.

"Yes, ma'am." Lennox shook away her nerves and put her hands to work, checking to see where she was needed most. Sparrows grew accustomed to the sight of bloody, wounded soldiers and learned how to pray in faith for them. Though, even with prayer, some were still lost. That was when they had to trust in God even more. Lennox constantly quoted "even if He doesn't" in her heart and mind. His ways were higher. Sometimes it was hard for her to remember that, but she tried.

Oliver continued to help Easton while Sky stayed by Lennox's side. Lennox combined the knowledge gleaned from observing her mother's nursing skills with her own extensive training gained the past few months and helped where she could. She moved to a surly young man who looked to be in his early twenties.

"Can you bring me a medical kit?" she asked. Sky nodded and ran to get the supplies.

"What's your name?" She looked into the injured young man's dimming, pale gray eyes. After all her training, she knew she needed to keep him talking. He looked like he was fading fast.

"Here." Sky put the tray of medical supplies on a rolling table next to her.

She whispered, "Find one of the lead medics."

Sky nodded and ran to find one.

"Al-ex, my…name's… Alex." Small gurgles broke his breathing.

She quickly put on surgical gloves and cut through his uniform with medical scissors, finding a bullet wound near his abdomen. She grabbed gauze and tried to stop the blood from gushing out of the quarter-sized hole. Lennox swallowed hard and focused.

"Hi, Alex. My name's Lennox." She tried to hide her urgency and managed a smile. The metallic smell of blood crept in as she breathed.

She reviewed the procedures she learned these past months and concentrated on the advice the lead medics gave everyone—stay calm, level-headed, and in command of your own senses. Lives were at stake. Lives were *always* at stake. Lennox took charge of her senses and used them all to care for Alex.

He struggled to talk. "I ha-ve..." he gasped. His eyes rolled back and his body convulsed. Beads of sweat formed on his skin and his face turned a sickly yellow.

Lennox wanted to panic. The old Lennox would have, but that version of her no longer existed. She allowed herself to be more than she ever thought she could be. She held the bandage tight and prayed for the battered soldier before her... this man she hardly knew.

If he were destined to live, God would be the one to bring him through. Her job involved doing whatever she could to help.

One of the lead medics approached the other side of the bed and lifted Lennox's hands to see the wound. "I will take it from here, Lennox. Good work."

Lennox allowed the lead medic's hands to replace her own and held her hands by her shoulders, taking deep, deliberate breaths. She watched her superior's movements.

Sky stood beside her. "Is he going to make it?"

"I hope so," she replied with her hands held up. She walked to a temporary sink that was rigged to allow water access via a faucet. She took off her gloves and threw them in the biohazard waste bin that sat next to the sink. Placing her hands under the running water, she scrubbed off the blood that managed to find her wrists. She looked around. All the wounded Sparrows were tended to. Most were in stable condition.

Medics wheeled Alex behind the plastic curtains of the Operating Room and attached monitors to his body. One read his heartbeat. It reminded Lennox of Kira— her high school best friend. She looked away. Kira's frail body was too broken and never stood a chance after the prom attack. She hoped Alex's fate would be different. Not one Sparrow had died... yet. It was a good day.

Sky walked Lennox to her room so she could change. She had to get the sticky blood off before she could eat.

Little Clover was bundled up on the top bunk. Lennox stretched on her tip-toes and brushed Clover's blonde hair back, tucking her blanket more securely with her other hand.

"Goodnight, Clover," she whispered, balancing back on her feet.

Clover had adjusted well to Sparrow City. She never mentioned her brother, but Lennox knew that deep down Clover must feel pain from the damage Thompson caused. After all, if not for him, Clover would have never dealt with such sorrow...at least... not alone, anyway. Lennox still could not imagine betraying her own family like he had. Clover deserved better.

Lennox looked closer and saw that Grizzly managed to get on the top bunk. The old German Shepherd let out a quiet moan while curled in a ball at Clover's feet. Lennox was convinced that Clover had replaced her as the dog's favorite—which was okay. She would do anything to keep Clover happy.

"How'd you get up there, Grizz?" Lennox whispered. Grizzly stared with soft brown eyes and then let out a small whine before closing them. "I guess you had a rough day, too."

Lennox threw on a new shirt over her undershirt and then walked out of the room.

Sky waited for her right outside the door. He had tied the arms of his jumpsuit around his waist and his white undershirt revealed his muscular, crossed arms. He leaned against the tunnel wall.

"Thanks for helping me, back in the ward," Lennox said full of gratitude.

Sky gave her the reassurance she needed just by the way he looked at her. His confident eyes reminded her that she knew exactly what she was doing.

"It was the least I could do," he replied with sincerity.

Peace and quiet finally fell over the halls. Children slept and the ward slowly fizzled back to normal as urgency vanished. All patients were in stable condition—even Alex. Lennox sighed. Everyone would be okay, and okay was better than what it could have been.

Sky's face looked urgent.

"What is it?" she asked.

"I overheard some things from the team that came in." He tensed his arms and pressed his body harder against the wall. Something more than the common influx of injured Sparrows in the ward consumed him. Something had changed. Something major happened.

"Sky, what did you hear?" Lennox held her right hand on her left elbow. She peered past the strong facade he maintained for everyone else.

Sky stood straight, pausing for a brief second. Surely contemplating the words in his head. "Our hometown. Ahab hit our hometown, Lennox."

Oh no, Pop. He's there, alone.

Lennox perceived the real source of Sky's worry. Pop's wheelchair surely made him an easy target, especially if Ahab knew his relation to her and Sky.

The Regime targeted family members of the Sparrows to draw them out of Sparrow City. No one was off limits—not the old, weak, nor children. Sky's grandfather would be no exception. He had stayed behind to help others escape the terror that trickled through the country.

Sky carried on with his concerns. "I am sure Pop didn't flee. You know him. He's stubborn as a mule. He'd never leave a man behind." Sky rubbed his chin. "Do you think they'd clear me to check on him?"

Lennox's heart sank. "I am not sure. We haven't even finished our training and you know how Easton feels about sending anyone out too soon. They'll dispatch a team and they'll find Pop. I'm sure of it."

Sky bit his lip and nodded. Lennox thought she saw tears in his eyes, but he sucked in a quick breath and changed the subject. "I guess we should eat." He popped his knuckles and walked toward the Dining Hall.

"Sky, we can talk about it more if you want while we eat. I will even go with you to ask Easton." She worried for him. "Maybe I am wrong. Maybe she'll let you go." Lennox cleared her throat, walking faster to keep his pace.

He hurt. She hurt for him, too. She would give anything… risk anything… to go back in time and hug her parents, to be with them one second longer. She wanted to give Sky the chance she never got.

Sky applied his brave front and squared his shoulders. "Nah, forget it. You're probably right. They'll send a team to get him."

He slowed down when they arrived at the doorway. Hungry medics filled the Dining Hall. Lennox and Sky grabbed a tray of prepared food and sat down on one of the long metal benches in the long, narrow cafeteria.

Sky countered Lennox's worried glances with small smiles and silence. Lennox suspected his mind was preoccupied with thoughts of their hometown and Pop. Lennox also worried for Pop. The only thing to do was trust God. *Trust God* constantly ran through her mind and heart.

She took small bites of her sandwich. Sky pushed his food away. The plastic tray skidded across the metal table. Lennox flinched back. Her eyes darted to him. He never behaved this way.

"You know what… I'm not hungry." He threw his elbows on the table to rest his forehead against his palms. He pressed them hard against his face.

Lennox wanted to say something… do something… *anything* to make Sky feel better. She wanted to take away the despair she knew he felt inside, but words failed her.

Chapter 7

Training started in the lab the next morning. This was where the scientists created the Sparrow technology they utilized in the field.

Lennox still noticed Sky's tension. He tightened his jaw and his shoulders were drawn. He hadn't let go of the idea of checking on Pop. She didn't blame him. She felt the same.

Sky shifted his weight from one foot to the other as he waited for the scientists to lecture. Lennox stood beside him with fellow recruits scattered around. She scanned the science lab.

The blue serum that was used in Sparrow ammunition filled several tall cylinders. The see-through liquid mesmerized her as it danced, floating up then back down in the transparent tubes. She wondered how long the scientists experimented on the serum before it worked. With just one drop, it brought a grown man down to the ground. It was not lethal, but it certainly made him helpless. It was designed to give the enemy a chance to know God, and that's what Lennox truly wanted.

She wanted men and women to know God as she knew Him. The bullets stopped them, Sparrows locked them away, and God worked on their hearts if they allowed Him. Lennox learned God was a God of second chances and—in her case—third and fourth chances. She prayed for her enemies as the Word of God instructed. She just hoped they would come to Christ because, without Christ, they were all lost.

Lennox looked away from the tubes and saw a pair of identical motorcycles. The two-wheeled machines were impeccable—black glossy paint and leather seats to fit two riders. Lennox knew Sky would get a kick out of getting to ride one, so would she.

A scientist with vibrant red hair walked to where Easton stood. He wore a white lab coat over the gray Sparrow jumpsuit. Easton introduced him.

"Recruits, this is Dr. Max McCabe, one of our lead scientists. It's his creations that you have been using during training. He and his team are working diligently on new technology to help us in the field. Today, we will learn about some of the new tech his team has made. Listen closely."

Max had the lightest shade of green eyes Lennox had ever seen. He spoke, his words eager and earnest. His strong Irish accent matched his appearance.

"We have created the motorcycles to be absolutely silent and will get you wherever you need to go without the worry of someone hearing your entrance or exit. The Vanishers, on the other hand, will make you invisible to the naked eye. The tech only lasts for a short time, though... long enough for you to get out of Sparrow City undetected, but not much farther. You will have to wear the helmet attachment still for vital reading and seeing through the cloaking mechanism. We can't have Sparrows running into each other, now can we?" He laughed awkwardly.

A female scientist dressed in the same white lab coat as Max walked to the motorcycles. She wore her short, shiny black hair slicked behind her ears. She smiled, looking at the recruits.

"All you have to do to activate the Vanisher is press this button when you are on the bike. The tech that makes you invisible will form around you, making the bike and rider virtually impossible to detect... except for those with Sparrow helmets, as Max has already said."

She pressed the button. The technology formed a sphere over the motorcycle, making it completely invisible. The look of satisfaction on her face was undeniable.

"Impressive, is it not?" she smiled.

"Definitely impressive, Sia. Good work." Easton gave a nod and smile to both scientists.

Max held up a finger and scurried forward. "Oh! And I forgot to mention the specialized tires. They're 'all-terrain.' Sand, mud, rock, grass—you name it! These tires can maneuver it." He smiled wide and tapped the front wheel on one of the bikes.

"Yes, I have seen these tires before in the field. They're outstanding, Max." Easton smirked at his child-like countenance. He looked like he lived, breathed, and slept science. "Why don't you tell them about the new Kev technology?" Easton pointed to the table full of small silver discs.

"Ah, yes!" Max picked a disk up, holding it high for every recruit to see. "This here is science at its finest. You've heard of Kevlar? Well, this is a bulletproof technology—carbon nanotubes that are flexible, lightweight, and chemically inert. Much like the dome that covers Sparrow City. It will virtually protect you from everything... bullets... blades... hail... "

Max pulled Lennox forward. "See?"

He pressed the silver disk onto her suit and it formed a thin layer of technology over her jumpsuit.

"Virtually weightless, sustainable protection. You, of course, will still need to attach the helmets, but the great thing is the nanotubes will automatically seal off the—"

"These are only prototypes." Sia stepped in and deactivated the disk, removing it from Lennox's suit. She held it firmly between two fingers as she held it up for everyone to see. She gave a serious glance. "Still working out some malfunctions." She glowered at Max and put the disk back with the others.

"Well... yes. A few minor adjustments could be made. They're *very* close to perfect." Max smiled back at her, folding his hand together.

Lennox thought of how interesting it would be to

work with both of them. The pair seemed to aggravate one another.

Max picked up another piece of technology but was interrupted by Cameron, the daughter of Sparrow City's founder. She walked into the lab and smiled the smallest smile imaginable. It was almost non-existent. Her face looked worn and her Sparrow suit was creased. When did the leader last sleep?

Soon the recruits whispered among themselves about Cameron's arrival.

"What's she doing here?"

"This is the first time I have ever seen her in person."

"She looks upset."

"Something bad must have happened."

Cameron took a quick breath, ignoring the whispers. "Listen up. Another wave just hit the eastern shoreline. If the tsunamis keep coming, there will be nothing left on that side of the country. The Regime will obliterate everything to secure Ahab's reign." Cameron pressed a button to reveal images.

Max, the red-haired scientist, looked at the projected holograms that were in the middle of the lab.

"He won't have much left to reign if he keeps that up." He pointed to the moving holograms. "The GWS is growing more powerful and disrupting more than just our weather. I've been studying the impact on our atmosphere for months. If you look closely, you will see it is also deteriorating the ozone layers beyond repair. The atmosphere just can't take it. Too much disruption in the natural weather patterns means something worse than the GWS will come." Max squeezed his freckled face together and shook his head violently back and forth.

"Please explain to the recruits," Easton said. Again, everything turned into a lesson.

Lennox discerned it was because Easton took full responsibility for what happened to the recruits and wanted to give them every chance to be better, stronger, and wiser for battle.

Sia answered, "Best case scenario? Loss of oxygen, loss of water supply, solar flares, and unstoppable meteors. Think of the planet without our ozone layer, without our atmosphere neatly in place. Everyone will need suits to survive, and suits may not even be enough. It will be as if we are on another

77

planet entirely."

There would never be enough suits to go around. Even if there were, there was not enough time to distribute them to everyone. Millions of captives and survivors were scattered around the nation—all around the world. How would they get to them all?

"And what's the worst case scenario, Max?" Easton tilted her head as she listened.

The recruits remained still as statues as they listened too. They were about to face that very danger.

"No one will live to see the worst case scenario." Max said, looking around to see everyone's reaction. They all looked to each other for courage. They would stop it before it ever got that far.

After the lesson in the lab, the recruits returned to the training room to finish out their last hour before lunch.

Sky approached Easton's office that sat to the right side in the training room. It was just a desk and two silver chairs—one in front of the desk and one behind.

Lennox watched a few feet away as Sky sat down in the available chair and asked the question she knew lingered in his heart. She could tell the conversation was not going as Sky had planned. Easton's methodical system of training and orientation before battle kept her from saying "Yes" to his request.

"It's too dangerous. The Regime is camped right outside." Easton folded her hands, placing them on the desk. "Sky, the best thing you can do for your grandfather is get fully trained before stepping onto the battlefield."

"Yes ma'am I understand that, but Ahab and his men are shooting to kill, and the GWS is destroying everything in its path," Sky said.

"You'd be risking your life to rush out there." Easton did not give in.

"By taking my time, I'm most likely risking Pop's life," Sky rebutted.

"I know you feel that way, but I assure you, when the scientists prepare more Vanishers—which will be soon—we will send out a team straight to your hometown. I promise."

Sky stood from the chair, lowering his head. "Yes, ma'am." As he moved away from the desk, Lennox heard the frustration in his next statement. "I just hope it's not too late."

Easton must not have heard because she tapped away at the keyboard on the computer at her desk.

Ace, standing a few feet away, overheard the conversation too. He placed his hand on his hips, watching. The warrior darted to Sky before Lennox could and threw his left arm around Sky's shoulders. Rather than add to the scene, Lennox decided she would talk to Sky afterward and let him cool off from the rejection.

Easton's choice made sense, but Sky's heart and intuition had to count for something. Lennox watched as Ace pulled Sky into the hall, away from it all. She hoped Ace could speak peace into Sky's life. The more voices of reason, the better. She wanted to be the pillar of strength Sky needed, but to do that, she had to be strong enough for the both of them. She had to get her mind right.

Lennox waited until Sky and Ace were farther down the hall before turning back around. The training room slowly emptied out for lunch, leaving her alone. She had her pick of the equipment. The dangling punching bag appealed to her first. There was just something satisfying about hitting a leather bag filled with sand.

Lennox put on a pair of sparring gloves and got started by fiercely hitting the black leather of the bag with all the force she could muster. She was frustrated with herself and with the news of their hometown. Even after all she had been through and all that God had done, fear still reared its ugly head, slithering into her heart, mind, and soul. It tried to stab away at her faith with every negative report. Lennox hit the bag harder and faster, thinking of the people she fought for.

With each alternating blow, she released a heavy breath. For her, it worked. It cleared her head and strangely enough, relaxed her nerves. She continued, one hit after the other.

Right... left... right.

The punching bag swung back and forth, and she took a step back. She rested her hands on her hips, looked up and breathed.

"I can do all things through Christ," she whispered to herself. Sometimes she needed the reminder. To be honest, she *always* needed the reminder. She couldn't do this... any of this... on her own.

"Hey, getting in some extra training?" Oliver

walked in.

Lennox stopped for a second. His face was clean-shaven and his hazel eyes were wide-awake from the coffee he held in his hand.

"Yeah, I'm just punching out some nerves, you know?" Lennox's fists throbbed.

"Yeah, I know." He smiled softly and sat on a steel bench that was pushed against the stone wall.

Lennox took the gloves off and sat by her brother. She looked at her red fists with a sigh and rested them on her lap, palms up. "Oliver, I'm afraid. My faith is constantly under attack. I should know better than to doubt, yet here I am worried... *scared*. Afraid for Pop, for Sky, for you, for me. How do you do it?"

Her brother huffed. "I get scared too. That's called being human. Don't you know I was afraid? Afraid of leaving you behind. Afraid of failing mom and dad. Faith is not the absence of fear, it is *believing*—even when you can't see, even when you're afraid. Faith is that constant war within that you must fight. Fear has to take a backseat to faith."

Oliver was as unwavering as ever. He was how she always saw him—strong and invincible. Her brother always made it better and always came through for her. He constantly reminded her of the need to fight for faith because it was a real battle and a real test. He was the perfect soldier. She hoped she would be, too.

"I just think people expect more of me, and I don't want to let them down. I don't want to let God down." Lennox brought her sore hands to her neck. She had survived the impossible and her faith had moved mountains. Why did she still feel so small?

"Just trust Him, and when the darkness seems closer to the light, pray. That's all we can do when there are no answers. You're the girl who stood, and you're also human. I'm here for you, always. We are going to get mom's locket back. And we are going to set off the tech dad hid inside of it. You just wait and see." Oliver tilted his head and smiled.

Lennox lowered her hand, giving a faint smile. "We're going to change everything."

She rested her head on Oliver's shoulder and fought the good fight for faith within her soul.

Chapter 8

Day turned to night. The physically easy morning session with the scientists was long gone. Lennox wiped her brow with a gray towel after another grueling night session with Easton. She waited for Sky.

Sky took a punch to the chin as he swung hard at his opponent. His partner threw jabs to his ribs and dodged. Sky matched the movements, ducking and swinging. A bell rang, signaling the end of the round.

Taking off his sparring gloves, Sky shook his opponent's hand and strolled toward Lennox. He had a priceless expression plastered on his face. His eyebrows were raised high and his lips pressed together. Lennox questioned whether she had ever seen him make that face before. It was unusual—especially after the news of their hometown. She appreciated seeing him semi-normal, but she wondered how deep he buried his real emotions. Though he did his best to pick up the broken pieces of his life and hide the hurting places from her... from everyone... she saw through the front.

He grabbed Lennox by the hand. "There's something I want you to see."

He smiled with deeply set dimples, his green eyes darkened by the blue shadows of the training room.

"Right now?" Lennox's heart hammered harder than it did from the workout.

"Yes, right now, but it's outside of the tunnels." His expression was that of an excited child. Lennox almost laughed.

"Okay." Lennox squinted, looking up at him and smiling more.

Where was he going to take her?

He held her by the hand as they walked past the hologram trees and the ward to the large double door entrance of Sparrow City. Sky scanned his hand and the heavy doors unlocked quietly.

The moonlit night spread before them. It was too beautiful not to notice. The clouds rolled away and it seemed every possible star was in sight. Their light flickered brightly. The moon gleamed, clearly visible as it rose above the hills and matched the stars' brilliant glow.

Sparrow City covered thirty square miles of pure country, with most of it underground. The only sign of human activity were the jets that sat in the distance.

Sky pulled Lennox by the hand gently, urging her forward.

"Where are you taking me?"

Lennox looked around, not wanting to get in trouble for leaving. Surely, Easton would not want them out too late. They needed to rest and prepare for the upcoming training sessions she had in store for them.

But… it would be nice not to have to think about it…. even for a few minutes.

Lennox let Sky pull her forward.

"Patience, you'll see in a minute. And don't worry, I got permission."

Sky knew her *so* well. Even the questions she didn't ask out loud, he answered. Lennox smiled and tilted her head to the side as Sky led her farther away from the doors. She glanced over her shoulder as they closed.

The darkness of night hid them from the Regime

on the other side of the dome that surrounded Sparrow City for protection. The dome's technology was so advanced that only the Sparrow scientists had it. It must have been created from God's divine inspiration. Nothing and no one could enter—except Sparrows equipped with the tech to do so. Occasionally the protective covering flickered, reminding Lennox of its presence.

Sky led her over two hills and stopped in a shallow valley between them. The grass had grown tall—almost to Lennox's knees—and swayed slightly in the wind. Lennox could not see anyone—not Regime soldiers, nor Sparrows. Nature enveloped her, drawing her closer. Their location was just far enough away to be secluded. It felt almost normal, as if normal still existed.

Normal was nice.

Silver moonlight danced over the sea of waving grass.

"What is this place?" Lennox asked, taking in the beauty of God's stunning creation.

"I found it when I was running a few days ago and wanted to wait for the perfect time to show you, but since everything is happening so fast, and there really is no perfect time..." Sky cleared his throat. "I thought now would have to be the time."

"What's so special about here? And perfect time for what?" The place undeniably beautiful, yes, but it looked like the other dips between the hills she ran during the day. Although, night had made it more stunning.

Sky bit his bottom lip. "Run your hands over the grass as you walk and you'll see." His smile lit up his face as he raised his eyebrows. His muscles flexed as he folded his arms, anticipating what he knew she would see.

Lennox stooped lower so her hands could reach the knee-high grass. She walked slowly, tracing over the soft green blades. She watched in awe as hundreds of fireflies lifted themselves into the sky. The soft glow of yellow light filled the air, dimming, and then relighting. Fireflies surrounded her and she gazed at them as they flew around her. They fluttered in the silvery moonlit sky, glowing yellow. The tiny creatures' unique beauty uplifted her. They calmed her nerves as anxiety gave way to peace. As they calmed her soul, they reminded her that there were still things on earth that showed the goodness of God, even in the darkness. After all, stars shined brightest in the darkness. She would shine brightest in the darkness too.

Oh! How she wished deeply for it to be a normal day with Sky—like the days before everything changed. Just another day after school, with Kira and her parents. Simple, memorable days that she should have appreciated more.

With her head lifted up, she said, "Sky, this is incredible! How is this even possible? Don't the fireflies…"

Sky had tears in his eyes. Sky never cried, not really. He cupped both of her heated cheeks in his strong hands.

"I know that the world is coming to an end, and there will be things out of my control, but I promise you, Lennox, I will do everything in my power to keep you safe." He stood straight and wiped the tears that fell from his eyes with his right thumb.

"I know you will, Sky. We're best friends. I will always have your back too." Lennox wrapped Sky in a hug. "We have to stick together." She paused and leaned closer to his ear. "I don't want to do this without you," she whispered.

He pressed his forehead to hers. "I can't do this without you."

Lennox held on to his hand as the fireflies began to settle, but her heart was far from settled. It raced from Sky's closeness. Amidst it all, she couldn't help the way he made her feel.

"Do you think we can sit out here for a while?" Lennox started to lower herself to the ground, not wanting to leave just yet.

"Of course." Sky slowly sat down beside her. "So what do think about all of this?"

"I don't know. I do my best to trust God. Sometimes it's still hard and I question myself. I just want to help everyone I can… so, I'm ready for that part. You?" Lennox tore a blade of grass and twisted it in her fingers.

"I'm ready. I mean, as ready as anyone can be. Right now I'm torn about Pop. He needs me now more than ever… and I'm not there for him. I should've never left him behind."

Lennox saw through his tough exterior and straight

to the guilt that weighed him down. His eyes were windows to the pain he tried to hide.

"Pop would want you to be safe." She took his hand and folded it into hers.

Sky searched the pockets of his jumpsuit with his other hand. "I almost forgot, I drew this for you." He held out a folded piece of cream drawing paper, changing the subject again.

He was so dedicated to hiding his heartache. Lennox wished he wouldn't hide his feelings from her. Maybe he wanted to protect her from his concerns—his uncertainty. She surrendered to his change of subject to avoid exhuming fresh wounds.

"You drew something for me?" Lennox smiled.

Sky simply nodded and waited for her to unfold his masterpiece. He recently broke out of his artistic shell, no longer hoarding his drawings for himself. Lennox often watched him sketch and saw the tension in his face disappear. She understood the release art gave him. It freed him from so many burdens he bore for everyone else.

She opened one fold after the other until the last piece opened. The glow of night and Sparrow lights provided just enough light to see the drawing. Again, like the one that fell from his sketchbook while they were on the run, a picture of her came into view—except this time she was fully decked out in Sparrow gear. Every detail was perfected—even the Sparrow emblem on the sleeve was drawn with true photorealism. His sketch portrayed a determined face and a strong body, but Lennox's favorite part was the verse he wrote beneath her booted feet. It was Psalm 91:2, "I will say of the LORD, 'He is my refuge and my fortress, my God, in whom I trust.'"

Lennox tucked a loose strand of hair behind her ear. "Thank you. You have no idea what this means to me."

"No problem. I know you don't want to let anyone down, and I know how hard it must be to be the girl who stood with the expectation everyone places on you. God's got you." Sky nudged her with his shoulder. "I almost put verse 13, 'you will trample the great lion and the serpent', but then thought that just might put more pressure on you."

He jokingly winked and threw his arm over her shoulders, bringing her closer to his side. She rested her

SPARROW

head on top of his muscular shoulder and took in every second. She breathed in deep and exhaled slowly. This moment must be captured in a freeze frame on Lennox's heart because she had no idea what tomorrow held.

Outside Sparrow City, peace was rare and internal peace must be guarded. Moments like this were good for her soul to reflect on. She hoped that they would get the chance to come back to this place and relive this exact moment when the war ceased... if it ever ended... if they survived. She was now a soldier—a Sparrow. At the same time, she was just a girl that dreamed of one day living her life... with her best friend.

Chapter 9

Lennox lay in her bed, unable to sleep.

Again.

Her mind swam with thoughts of Sky, their friendship, and fireflies… all mixed with twinges of anxiety about Pop and the war. When she finally closed her eyes and quieted her mind enough to fall asleep, she tossed and turned. Her heart and mind still tried to figure it all out. It tried to cope with the reality that was soon to come.

The pit is dark, the only light coming from above is where Ahab stands, glaring down at her. Her heart hammering, Lennox watches, frozen. He shoves someone forward.

Mom!

Before Lennox can move to her mother's side, a

grunt draws her eyes up to Ahab. Another body falls, barely missing Mom as it lands beside her. Dad's twisted body is covered in bruises so pronounced on his pale skin she can make them out even in this dim light. Her breathing quickens.

She is out of the pit. How did she get out? She doesn't have time to question it. Ahab stands before her now. No pit... no walls surrounding them. With his left hand, he rips the locket from her neck while his right hand wraps around her neck.

Air! She kicks, her feet lift from the floor. She claws Ahab's arms.

He's gone.

Another takes his place. From the darkness, Thompson emerges, a branding iron in his hand. Lennox struggles as faceless soldiers restrain her. Thompson thrusts the red-hot D onto her bare flesh. Pain screams up from the site of the brand and out her mouth, but Thompson only laughs. He vanishes as a Prowler raises a whip. She braces for the first slash.

Fists clenched and elbows out, Lennox jabbed. Unlike the hardness of the training dummy, a soft, feathery culprit greeted her rage. A bead of sweat dripped down her face. Panting, Lennox opened her eyes. Her hands coiled into fists, twisting in the sheets. She blinked, her heart still racing.

Safe. Underground in Sparrow City. *Safe.*

No Ahab… no Prowlers….

"I'm safe," Lennox panted.

Just another bad dream.

Sweat covered her body and pillow. She propped herself up on her elbows and caught her breath. The muscles in her arms were tight and sore. The memories burned in her mind like imprints in the sand. The fact that she may lose someone else she loved to the war she fought so hard against made her sick to her stomach. She had already lost too much—her mom, dad, and Kira—that was enough. There was so much to lose…so much to gain. She couldn't lose anyone else. She wouldn't lose anyone else, not if she could do anything about it.

Pulling the sweaty, cotton shirt from her back, she collapsed back onto her pillow.

With the knowledge of leaving soon, Lennox trained hard and consumed every ounce of instruction she could from Easton and the other instructors. She fought and concentrated so hard during the sessions that she did the maneuvers she learned during training in her sleep. Her muscles involuntarily went through the motions of her repetitive hours of fighting and dodging. Oliver told her that it was normal and that he experienced the same thing. After all, once you do something over and over again, it becomes second nature. Her brain was only doing what it had told her muscles to do time and time again while she was awake. She was physically stronger than she had ever been before and hoped her spirit was too.

She couldn't fall asleep again. Too many nerves. Too many fears.

She sat up and grabbed a tech screen from the stool beside her bed. Psalm 46 always calmed her, so she read, "God is our refuge and strength, an ever-present help in trouble. Therefore, we will not fear, though the earth give way and the mountains fall into the heart of the sea, though its waters roar and foam and the mountains quake with their surging."

She highlighted her favorite parts—the ones she could lean on in the time of trouble— parts that reminded her who He was and how all-powerful He was. She restated the verse in her own words to help them sink in.

"God is within her, she will not fall. He makes wars cease to the ends of the earth. He breaks the bow and shatters the spear. He burns the shields with fire."

God was within her and she would not fall... she could not fall... she could not fail. Too much was at stake. He would lead her in the fiercest of battles, and no matter what the odds looked like, God was stronger. Not even the Global Weather Simulator was greater. In her life, God had control.

Lennox wiped the sweat away and thanked God for reminding her who she was in Him. She could fight as long as God was on her side. She would trust Him. She had to.

Noise in the hall took her eyes away from the soft glow of the tech screen. The pit of her stomach told her something wasn't right. She felt it.

The clock read two a.m. She rolled the gray covers away and walked to her room's doorway. A tall muscular frame that was all too familiar crept down the hall.

Sky?

What was he doing this time of night? She decided to follow him.

She reached for her jumpsuit and slipped it on. Turning around in the doorway, she glanced at a sleeping Clover and Grizzly. She shoved on her boots and zipped up her suit, then walked into the hall.

The night guards had not made their rounds yet. She followed until he entered the Sparrow lab. Lennox quietly stood in front of the lab door as it slid shut. Scientists kept a record of everyone coming and going. How was she going to explain a two a.m. visit to the lab? Maybe he couldn't sleep either.

She pressed her hand against the screen, allowing the red line to scan her prints. The door opened and she saw Sky fully geared for battle. He was mounted on a Vanisher—the very Vanisher the scientists had just explained to them in training. He also had a Striker holstered to the side of the bike, along with another small Sparrow gun in the holster on his thigh. The wide sliding metal door opened to the outside, waiting for the exit of one lone soldier... waiting for Sky to leave her behind.

"What are you doing?" Lennox asked even though

she knew.

I can't believe it, she thought as her heart sank. She didn't know whether to be angry because he was leaving without telling her, or because he was leaving at all. Both sent blood rushing to her face with a consuming wave of heat.

Sky turned his head but refused to look her in the eyes. He chose not to answer the question.

"You're going to Pop, aren't you?" She inched closer to him, walking past the cylinders of blue serum. "*Seriously?* You weren't going to tell me? That's what last night was about, wasn't it? You were saying *goodbye*." Lennox shook her head. He said he couldn't do it without her, yet now he was willing to leave her behind? He infuriated her.

"I didn't want to get you involved. I wanted to protect you." Sky looked her straight in the eyes now.

Of course. Protector Sky.

She both admired him and despised him for trying to sneak away without telling her. She didn't want to be protected. She wanted the truth.

"Sky, you can't do this. As much as you think you are, you're not ready. What are you going to do if you run into soldiers… into *Prowlers*? The Regime is camped right outside, all around."

"I know." He furrowed his eyebrows and looked at the ground, clenching his jaw. He stared at the wall. Lennox knew for sure it was to keep her from seeing his emotions.

She reached for the Kevlar tech prototype on a stainless steel work table, along with a helmet. She stepped closer until she was a foot away from Sky. She considered the repercussions of his choice, soon to be her choice. She wavered between two options—stay and let Sky go alone, or go, and leave Oliver behind. Neither was acceptable, but her love for Sky triumphed.

Against her better judgment, she got on the back of his bike. She cared too much for Sky to let him go alone. She couldn't lose him too.

Sky looked over his shoulder, shocked at Lennox sitting behind him. She didn't understand his shock. He should've known she wouldn't let him go alone.

He shook his head. "What are you doing?"

"Going with you." Lennox activated the tech and placed the helmet on her head.

"Lennox, you can't." Sky shook his head in

protest. "Get off the bike." He pressed the handles of the bike harder to stabilize it.

"No." Lennox shook her head. "I'm not letting you leave alone. If you go, I go."

Lennox wouldn't give in. Through thick and thin, she always had his back… no matter what.

"It's too dangerous," Sky warned.

"That's not going to work." Lennox remained on the bike. Nothing he could say or do would persuade her to get off.

"We'll get in trouble." Sky said, still trying.

"I know." She remained immovable.

"Oliver will be furious." He looked at her over his shoulder, giving her one more chance to get off. His eyes begged her to let him go alone.

"I know."

Oliver *would* be furious. What was she doing? What was she thinking? She hated to disrespect Easton's authority and leave without telling Oliver, but how could she let Sky go on a mission alone? She couldn't. She wouldn't.

Sky kicked the bike's kickstand up with his right boot. Lennox held tight to his waist as he accelerated the silent engine. The door slid shut with their exit.

The thought of making Sky turn back crossed Lennox's mind, but she knew he would go without her if she did. She couldn't let that happen. She hoped their risk didn't cost them more than a reprimand.

The motorcycle picked up speed, rolling over the hills. Sky positioned the bike smoothly through a small opening in the trees. They passed through the barrier of Sparrow City, exiting the very dome that kept them safe. Sky maneuvered the bike into the densely wooded area.

Regime soldiers glanced their way. Lennox's heart threatened to jump right out of her chest. She felt vulnerable now that the dome was behind them and unprotected earth stretched before them. One soldier stood in the clearing, tilted his head, and moved a step forward. A chill ran down Lennox's spine. She waited for him to investigate—waited for the onslaught of bullets. The soldier shrugged and sat back down.

Thank you, God! Lennox praised. She didn't want to think of what would happen if they were attacked by the Regime.

Now, to make sure Pop was okay and return before

they got into too much trouble.

Chapter 10

The early morning sun rose above the horizon, casting a breathtaking glow of orange and pink upon the earth. Several hours had passed since their departure from Sparrow City. Lennox spent most of that time praying silently—praying the Vanishers wouldn't give out at an inopportune time, praying Oliver would understand why she'd felt compelled to leave, praying the unauthorized trip would prove a worthwhile endeavor.

Lennox watched the tech flicker around their feet. Within minutes, their invisibility disappeared altogether. They were already AWOL. Now they were fully exposed.

Lennox sighed softly. What were they doing?

"At least the Vanishers lasted long enough to get us past those Regime soldiers."

She still couldn't believe they had left.

"Yeah," Sky said so low that Lennox barely heard him.

The motorcycle swerved through the trees, missing branches all along the way. Sky was not afraid of speed and he drove the bike faster than Lennox liked.

"The hardest part is over." Sky said in reference to getting out of Sparrow City alive.

Lennox disagreed. The hardest part awaited them. Lennox felt it in her heart. It made her feel uneasy.

Sky sped toward the coordinates. Lennox already had her hands latched around his waist, but she gripped them firmly together so they would not slip apart. Her body leaned with his as he turned. He swerved the bike to a halt, making Lennox squeeze him even tighter around his mid-section.

He put his feet on the damp earth. The land appeared to have recently experienced a flood. Thick mud caked the tires.

"We'll move faster on the road."

Sky moved the bike up a small slope. A winding road stretched before them. It was filled with abandoned vehicles. A minivan with a stick-figure family decal on its back windshield was a reminder of possessions that were left behind. Lennox wondered what the family who left the minivan behind had to run from. Perhaps it was Regime soldiers or drones. It did not matter. No one was left. Only traces of them remained. Everything was a mere remnant now, and material possessions no longer mattered.

Their surroundings weighed heavily on Lennox's heart. No amount of passing time could make her forget what she saw. Her continued faith in God kept her moving, even through the loss, heartache, and questions. She hoped her testimony of how God brought her through would help someone else move forward, despite despair. Despair could be a catalyst to drive someone to Christ. He would be hope in their desperation. He would be their light in their darkest hour. Lennox kept her eyes on Him. She had felt the weight of loss herself. She understood it. She did not want to become numb to the lost.

The miles to Sky's old house were tumultuous. Rain poured from the sky as the bike rolled over the wet asphalt and past twisted trees and animal carcasses. The smell of tar, plowed soil, and burned wood filled the air. Travel was excruciating. They saw the Regime's increased destruction through the mist and fog. Buzzards flew in circles above them.

Rolling up to the farmhouse, Sky slowed the bike to a stop and kicked the kickstand into place. He hastily dismounted and sprinted over smoldering wood.

The rain was steady as Sky ran to his childhood home. The red door that Pop had refurbished and installed a few years ago bore the spray-painted symbol for Defiers. Sky ran his hand over the painted *D* with a circle drawn around it. The *D* that stained the door symbolized what the fight was really about, a battle for the hearts of men.

The warm and inviting house Lennox remembered was no more. The door frame was almost all that stood unscathed. The rest of house was splintered and concave in the middle.

Lennox forced her body off the bike and maneuvered herself through the debris. Sky climbed over one of the blown out windows next to the door frame and walked into what used to be the kitchen. Lennox followed.

The stove stood perfectly in its place as if the surrounding house were untouched. Even the cast iron skillet that was left on the burner contained blackened hot water cornbread. Lennox expected the worst and looked around for remnants of a wheelchair—the remnant of Pop.

Sky saw the skillet. He walked over to it, touching the handle and shaking his head. "He didn't know they were coming."

"I know." Lennox was careful as she made her way to Sky. "We'll keep looking,"

Lennox hoped that Pop had made it out. She didn't want Sky to see him if he hadn't.

"This doesn't make any sense. Pop would have known." Sky's eyes met Lennox's. "He was too cautious *not* to have known. They have him... they have to have him." His boots crunched the ruin underneath him.

"Then we will find him." She offered a glimmer of hope.

He bit his bottom lip to keep focused and nodded his head. "I'm going to search the back."

"I'll keep searching for clues up here," Lennox said.

Sky walked to the torn-down back end of the house. Everything Pop owned—the pictures on the walls, the pristine antiques—all were scattered along the ground in pockets of rubble.

Lennox looked in what used to be the den area and saw a twisted up wheelchair under heaps of wood and ash. She took a deep breath and exhaled. Her nerves shook and her heart thumped. An old leather boot that was buried slightly lay beside the wheelchair. Lennox immediately knew that Pop was somewhere close. She had seen Pop lace up those very same boots every morning when she stayed with him after Oliver left. They were weathered with the soles worn from before Pop's injury. Pop said they were his favorite pair of boots because they reminded him of when he could walk.

Oh, God.

"Please let him be alive." Lennox searched the surrounding land for the other boot or signs of Pop.

She walked a little farther. She found the other boot underneath ash and burned wood.

Ba-bum, ba-bum, ba-bum.

Her heart hammered in her ear drums so loud it sounded like a bass drum. The boot was still laced neatly on Pop's foot. She hurriedly got on her knees and removed the rubble that lay on top of him.

She saw it—her soul recoiled as her gut twisted.

Pop. A bullet wound to his right temple.

Lennox sank to her knees. Through a veil of weeping, she cleared the ash from his face and closed his eyes. She reached for his stiff hand, wrapping it between her own as she sucked in sobbing breaths.

Sky. Oh, Sky! What is he going to do?

Lennox looked around desperately, trying to find the courage to call out for Sky… to tell him the unbearable news.

She released Pop's wrinkled hand and set it down gently at his side. As she stood, she saw Sky standing directly behind her. Her body blocked Pop's face from view.

"Sky." She barely managed a whisper. She shifted to the left, clearing Sky's line-of-sight to his grandfather.

"Pop!" In a heartbeat, he was there. "Pop… No… Oh, Pop!" He lifted Pop's shoulders off the ground and cradled him in his arms. "Pop… I'm so sorry… I never should have left you." Tears wet his face, his voice was mournful. "I never should have left you!"

His screams penetrated Lennox's heart to the core.

She knelt beside him.

"Sky, I'm so sorry."

Tears pooled in her own eyes. Sky just kept shaking his head "No" as he rocked Pop's lifeless body back and forth. She watched helplessly as Sky's world crashed down all around him… all around them. In a blink of an eye, their world fell apart all over again.

They were too late.

Chapter 11

After what felt like hours, Sky finally lifted his face from Pop's neck and looked at Lennox. "We have to bury him, give him a proper resting place."

Sky gently laid Pop's body to the ashen earth. He wiped his fallen tears away, no longer trying to hide his emotions.

"I will do whatever you need me to do." Lennox waited for Sky to form words.

He rubbed his face with the back of his hand, wiping away the sweat. "His grave will need a marker."

Sky's green eyes looked so heavy and full of guilt, Lennox empathized with him. It wasn't that long ago when she sat on top of a silo, wondering where God was in it all. At least Sky had not run like she had.

"I will make a cross out of some wood from the house." Lennox stepped away to gather the supplies she needed.

Sky breathed out a heavy breath. "Do you think we

can find a picture of him and me?"

"Of course, I will find one."

Lennox moved to the pile of photos she saw earlier hidden behind shattered glass. She dug through the broken frames, one by one.

Pop loved his photos. He had framed pictures everywhere in the old farm house—dozens of him and Sky. It was easy for Lennox to dig one up. She pulled a small, four-by-six inch copper frame up that held a precious memory. It was a picture of Sky sitting on Pop's lap. In the photo, Sky couldn't have been any older than five.

Lennox wiped the ash off the cracked frame and gathered splintered wood to make a cross. She found some twine to weave the two pieces of thin wood together. It wasn't perfect, but Pop would have called it beautiful.

Lennox took her findings to Sky. He dug a shallow grave with the shovel he found in a nearby shed. It was just big enough for Pop and was near the trees that were away from the burned rubble.

"Will you help me move him?" Sky placed the shovel on the ground. He had a dirtied white bed sheet ready to transport Pop.

Lennox nodded, placing her items down. She walked to Pop, who lay only a few feet away. Sky grabbed Pop under the arms, and Lennox held on to his feet, working with Sky to place Pop on the sheet. Lennox lowered her head as she helped Sky carry his slain grandfather to the shallow grave he had dug.

How could any of this be turned for good?

She gathered the cross, shovel, and picture, and then joined Sky at the gravesite. She lay everything down except the shovel and began to pick up the disturbed soil to place on top of Pop.

"I'll do it." Sky reached out for the shovel.

Sky sucked back tears with every layer of dirt that covered Pop. When he finished, Lennox put the cross in place. She handed Sky the picture she found. He dropped the shovel aside.

"Thank you," he said, taking the picture out of the antique frame. He admired it for a moment, and then folded it to put in his pocket.

Crouching down, Sky ran his hand over the dirt.

"Pop, you were a good, God-fearing man. A good father... a good grandfather. I don't know who I would have been without you... and... one day, Pop, I promise you... I will be as good of a man as you were. I love you." Sky swallowed hard. He stood back up. "I guess we should head back." Sky wiped away his tears and moved toward the bike.

Lennox stared down at the soil through teary eyes. "Goodbye, Pop. Thank you for taking me in when you didn't have to. Watch over us." Lennox lifted her eyes. "God, help us all."

She ran to Sky and wrapped him in a hug. He slumped into her embrace and sobbed, releasing every bit of emotion that he had held back for so long.

Lennox prayed for him. It was all she knew to do. No words could make it right. No words could go back in time and stop it all from happening. Prayer made the difference when she couldn't.

"Lord, give him the peace that passes all understanding."

Only God could heal his broken heart, and only God could give him the peace he needed—she knew that firsthand.

As she prayed, a lone red sparrow landed on top of the cross that served as the grave marker. The bird's head tilted side-to-side.

Lennox released Sky and took his hands. His emotions were written all over his face.

"Look." She pointed to the sparrow.

A flood of tears welled in Sky's eyes. He gnawed on his lip as he focused on the red bird.

It sat on the cross, unmoving... unshaken by the two humans that towered beside it. Then, it chirped a song that sounded beautiful, hopeful even. The melody echoed as the wind blew, yet everything stood still. The breeze was felt but not seen. The red sparrow flew away and headed east.

Lennox exhaled, knowing that sometimes God sent signs so subtle that one could miss it if he were not listening... seeking.

"We should head back," Sky said with his head down. Had they missed the point of the sign the bird gave? Was it a sign at all?

"Okay," Lennox agreed.

She wasn't going to argue with him right now. They should get back. She just didn't want him to hide his pain to protect her. She wanted to help him, to let him know that everything was going to work out. They would see Pop again just as she would see her parents again... one day.

Sky turned and held up his hand, then pressed his pointer finger to his lips.

"You hear that?" His eyes surveyed the land around them.

Lennox listened closely. A strange buzzing noise filled the air around them. It sounded like a bee that flew too close to her ear.

"What is that?" Lennox was searching for the sound's source when she saw Sky draw the handgun from his thigh holster.

A black drone, no bigger than a man's fist, hovered a few feet in front of them. Sky pulled the trigger, sending the miniature drone tumbling down. He inched closer to the fallen drone, kneeling when he reached the tiny, twisted machine.

"Ours?" Lennox hoped Sparrows had sent out the drone to assess the damage.

"Theirs," Sky said point-blank. "The Regime knows we're here now."

Chapter 12

Lightning laced across the sky. Thunder cracked behind them. The storm seemed to chase the rogue teenage soldiers as they raced to Sparrow City.

Lennox counted the seconds between the lightning and thunder under her breath like her dad had taught her to when she was young. She would always smile in delight when her dad counted and pointed up when the thunder was close. She would giggle as the ground rumbled beneath her. "One Mississippi...two Mississippi...three Mississippi..." She thought it was magic the way her father knew right when thunder would shake the earth. The older she got, the more she understood the science behind it, but pretended to believe in her father's superhero likeness. It made him happy, so it made her happy.

I wish you were here, dad.

She counted. "One...two..." There was no giggling now, no happy laughter, no cuddling next to her father's side as the thunder roared. The storm was way too close. "Coincidence?" Lennox yelled.

"I don't know!" Sky shouted. He looked to the river rising beside them.

Coincidence or not, they were in trouble. The water below swallowed the earth as more water bled down from above.

"Sky, don't!" Lennox said too late.

He ran the bike over a bridge above the water. The rising river smashed into the side of the ancient looking conduit, threatening to collapse it and suck it in. A violent rush of muddy water swept the support beams of the bridge away. Sky and Lennox were swept away with it.

The water submerged her in its grasp before she could take her next breath. She thrashed her arms and kicked her feet to reach the surface. The bulletproof technology did nothing to keep the water out. Gasping for air, she turned to find Sky. He was downriver, ten feet away. Too far.

She fought to get to him as he fought to reach her. The water sucked her back under and tossed her body in its grip, flipping her upside down. The strap to the

Striker twisted around her neck, choking her more. She fumbled to loosen it under the water. For a split second, she saw stars falling in the blackness of the water.

It was beautiful.

It was dangerous.

It was death.

Her gun disappeared down river and her struggle diminished. She stopped fighting against the water. She let go of the life that remained in her, relinquishing herself and her body to God's hands. Flashes of her mother and father teaching her how to swim crossed her mind. They always told her that the number one rule to swimming was "don't panic."

Everything turned black and her body grew tired. She heard her father's voice yell like when she was a child.

"Fight, Lennox. Swim!"

A light pierced the darkness. Flickers of sun rays danced on the river's surface. She refused to give in to the undertow that dragged her further under. She reached for the light and a hand reached into the depth of the river, pulling her back up to life. It felt like a resurrection from darkness to light. The starry vision of a face was all she could make out.

"Lennox!" Sky yelled to reawaken her senses.

More stars, then focus.

She coughed up water and fought hard to swim again. Sky held on to her by her suit and pushed against the flood to reach the riverbank. Lennox choked on the water that invaded her lungs.

Sky reached the riverbank and shoved Lennox ashore. She threw off her helmet and coughed rigidly as she propped her body on her hands and knees, vomiting most of the water that sloshed in her stomach. Sky knelt beside her and coughed up his fair share of water too, yet he appeared more worried about Lennox than himself.

"You're okay, just get it out," Sky said, holding back her disheveled hair.

When Lennox finished heaving, she rolled on her back.

"You need to sit up and breathe. Just breathe." Sky helped Lennox into a sitting position.

"I'm—" She vomited more fluid. "…Okay." She let out more mouthfuls of fluid, then sucked in oxygen like it was as valuable as gold. To her, it was. She couldn't get enough of it. She felt the blood return to her face as her oxygen levels stabilized.

Sky held Lennox in his arms.

The bike was gone… their gear gone… *everything* gone. Just like that. In one fell swoop. The only weapon they had left was the gun strapped to Sky's thigh—if the water hadn't destroyed it. All Lennox had was the utility knife she kept in a secret compartment in her boot. What had they gotten themselves in to?

"Humph." Lennox couldn't believe they had even survived the flash flood. The river turned into raging white water just twenty feet from where they escaped.

She rested her head on Sky's chest. "We're in so much trouble." Lennox bit her bottom lip, watching the bike travel farther away without them, being tossed to and fro by the white water until it went under completely.

Sky held her closer. "I'm so sorry." Lennox felt his chin tremble as he pressed it into her hair. "I never meant for any of this to happen." He paused. "I never should have let you come."

"You couldn't have stopped me, I made my own choice." Lennox hadn't blamed him.

"I know." His heavy breaths made his chest rise and fall against her cheek. "We should head back. It will take us longer now." Sky released her and rose to his feet.

Lennox stood and tried to wipe the caked mud from her hands. "Lead the way."

She gave her friend the opportunity to lead and allowed him to choose the best direction back.

Sky angled his head. "This way." His wet boots stuck to the earth, slinging mud upward with every step.

Wet boots rubbed Lennox's feet raw. The sheer weight of her soaked uniform made her muscles throb. Hopefully the sun would dry their suits soon.

So much for the Kev tech... must be one of the "kinks" Sia spoke of.

Sky pushed tree branches out of the way and held them back as Lennox passed. He was a gentleman, even in tragedy.

Lennox forced a smile. "Thanks."

"No problem." Sky returned to leading the way back to their new home. There was nothing left for him at his old one.

Lennox marched behind him. His shoulders were slumped and his head never lifted. Lennox caught the hint from the lack of small talk that Sky needed silence.

Rustling leaves caught her attention. Birds frantically flew out of the distant trees behind them. Sky held up his hand and drew his sidearm. Lennox stutter stepped behind him and pulled the knife from her boot, smirking at the blade.

Who am I kidding?

Nonetheless, she held it out and stayed behind Sky as he walked with his gun aimed. They heard voices.

Maybe five…six men. A dozen?

Chapter 13

A stream of blue lasers met Sky's chest.

Easton stood before Lennox and Sky with a team of eleven men behind her, including Oliver. Easton held down her weapon and pursed her lips. Lennox bit the inside of her cheek and lowered her knife. She avoided eye contact at all costs.

Oh no. We're in SO much trouble.

Oliver rushed out from the back, running straight to Lennox.

"I'm so glad you're okay!" he sighed, hugging her. Then his eyebrows furrowed and his face reddened as his nostrils flared. He held her shoulders and looked her in the eyes. "What were you two thinking?" He threw a glance to Sky. "You could have been killed!"

"I'm sorry," Lennox said, genuinely remorseful for leaving. Guilt weighed heavy on her heart. It was stupid... foolish... *selfish*... it was everything she didn't want to be. It wasn't the right choice, but she was glad she was with Sky when he needed her. She couldn't imagine him dealing with the loss of Pop alone. He might have never returned.

"Oliver, it's my fault Lennox left," Sky said, stepping forward. He twisted his mouth to the side and didn't say anything else.

"I know it's your fault. Lennox wouldn't leave on her own." Oliver shook his head.

"How'd you find us?" Lennox wanted desperately to take the fault away from Sky.

"We tracked you guys." Oliver clicked his finger against Lennox's suit. His face returned to normal behind his visor. "Where's Pop?"

Lennox's eyes found the dirt.

Poor Pop.

She raised her eyes back up to face the bitter truth. "Pop didn't make it." Lennox looked to Oliver then Easton.

Sky peered at Easton, and then shook his head. He walked off to stand by himself a few feet away. He crossed his arms and clenched his jaw, causing the tendons in his face to protrude. Lennox started toward him, wanting to console him, to wrap him in her arms and tell him everything was going to be okay, even though everything was not okay.

Oliver stopped her. "I'll go."

Lennox remained in place. "Okay."

She stood still and refused to look at Easton. She knew she had disobeyed and disappointed her, but Pop was gone now. There was nothing anyone could do. She would do it again for Sky if she needed to.

Easton breathed heavily. "I don't blame you guys for going. But I had orders I had to follow. They were orders to protect you, and that's what I was trying to do." She turned toward the Sparrows. "You guys go ahead and get the Humvees ready for transport." The Sparrows behind Easton turned around and walked through the trees.

Sky shouted. "The Regime doesn't fear us, you know!" He threw his hand around the back of his neck and paced. Both Lennox and Easton looked in his direction.

Oh no.

Was he going to explode? If he did, Lennox wouldn't blame him. She and Easton strained to better hear the discussion between Sky and Oliver.

Sky removed his hands from his neck and rested them at his side with balled up fists. "They. Don't. Fear. Us." Sky said again through gritted teeth.

"They don't have to." Oliver grabbed Sky's arm. "*This rage*, this need to avenge Pop will not bring healing. It will not bring peace. And I know the hurt is fresh. Trust me, I know. I know what it's like to want to take everything from them like they took from you. But they don't have to fear us. They will learn, very soon, to fear our God." Oliver let Sky's arm go. "You can't let the Regime take your heart. Not now. Not ever."

Sky lowered his head. "I know. I'm trying…"

"We'll get through this. All of us, together." Oliver raised a hand to Sky's shoulder. "I promise."

Oliver returned with Sky to where Lennox and Easton stood a few feet away.

Easton rubbed the back of her neck. "I'm very sorry, Sky. I wish things were different."

"Me too," Sky said, nodding to her. Easton nodded back an unspoken forgiveness.

"So now what? Have you come to take us back and discipline us?" Sky asked her.

She smiled. The silvery scar on her face curved. "No." She motioned for Lennox to come closer. "The team of Sparrows that came into the ward tracked down the locket. They were in y'all's hometown when they were ambushed."

Oliver held out a hologram message portal. "One of them found this." He handed the portal to Lennox. "It has a message on it for you... *for us*."

Lennox's heart beat faster as she held the portal in her hand.

A message. From who?

She set the device on the ground and pressed play. An image of her father appeared. She reached out for her brother's hand and squeezed it tight as their father spoke.

"I am sure both of you have many questions, and if you are seeing this, it means that your mother and I are not there to answer them for you. For that, I am sorry. We never meant to withhold the truth from the two of you. We only wanted to protect you. You see, early on, before either of you were even born, we were given a vision, a prophecy. At the time, we had no idea what the world would become, but the more we saw everything unfold, we knew what we had to do."

Their dad's hologram looked away and then back. "We knew this would be difficult for all of us, but we also knew there was a greater purpose. Oliver, we knew you would be special and brave beyond belief. We knew that if it ever came down to it, you would fight, and so we left you to your purpose."

Lennox looked at her brother. His eyes welled with tears. She saw him fight to keep every single one from falling. Their dad continued.

"Lennox..." The sound of her dad's voice speaking her name made her stiffen. She inhaled, trying to calm her heartbeats so that she would not hear the thud in her ears. "You were the one we knew would have a harder time with what would be our fates, and that is why we chose you to take the locket. We wanted to hand you a destiny that you might have otherwise refused, but we know your heart is to help others. And the locket will do that.

"Your fingerprint will remove a gold overlay on the inside of the locket to reveal a microchip. Get the microchip close enough to any hard drive in the Regime's main frame and the nanobytes will do the rest. They will set off a chain of events that will destroy the Regime from the inside out."

Lennox's eyes fell to the floor. Her parents were right. She probably would never have fought so hard without a true sense of purpose attached to the fight. She had to get the locket back from Ahab. She had to remember the real reason she fought.

Her dad's voice grabbed her attention again. "We love you both with all of our hearts. Be safe and know that God will get you both through this. I believe in the greater purpose He has for your lives." The volume of their father's voice increased when he said his final words. "Be brave."

The hologram dwindled away with the last message they would ever receive from their parents.

Could they really do this?

Sometimes Lennox still felt like a child—but she wasn't a child anymore, and it was time to put away childish things. Lennox closed her eyes for a brief second and opened them slowly while she processed the information she had just received.

She would be brave.

Lennox despised the Regime and what they did.

She had to steal the locket back before it was too late. It could change everything…It *would* change everything. Ahab enjoyed the game of cat and mouse—as long as he was the cat. For once, she would be the cat, and he'd be running from her.

Lennox curved her fingers around the message portal. "So you *are* going to let us go with you?"

Easton broke the ice first. "Oliver assured me that your and Sky's insubordination was an isolated incident. I choose to believe it was, too. I just need to know both of you will follow orders. It's imperative that I know I can count on the both of you." Easton shifted her gaze between Sky and Lennox.

"Yes ma'am," Lennox said without hesitation. She never wanted to disobey orders in the first place.

"Yes ma'am," Sky confirmed after a quick pause.

Easton spoke, "There's one more message you need to hear. General Eli wanted to share something with us before we head out on our mission."

Easton set the hologram message portal on the ground, pressing the play button before taking a step back. A life-size image of Eli—the head of Sparrows—appeared from the portal.

"You must be aware that this war is not only a physical battle, it is very much a spiritual one. Every part of you will be tested, tried. If a Prowler does get a hold of your mind, every part of your flesh will fight against your spirit. Your fears, failures, the darkest part of yourself will fight against you. You must fight back. I've seen too many good men get taken down. Prepare your hearts for what you are walking in to."

Eli's hologram flickered as he breathed heavy and shifted his weight. "You will be walking into enemy territory. You will see terrible, disturbing things. Don't let what you see reach your heart. Seek God in the valley. I believe in you... all of you. Captain Cameron and the scientists will assist you from Sparrow City in whatever you need. Go with God." Eli's hologram fizzled away.

Sky's warm hand brushed up against Lennox's cold fingers. He wrapped his hand around hers and squeezed tight. He had her back and she had his. *Always.*

The fight belonged to them now. They could do this. It was their destiny. Lennox and Sky had spent every waking moment in combat and medical training for months. They worked diligently to be as prepared as they could be for this war that they inherited. All the target practice and evasive hand-to-hand combat techniques were about to be put to the test.

"Let's get you two new gear back at the Humvee." Oliver motioned for them to follow him. Lennox swallowed hard and did so.

Was this really it? The time was now?

At the Humvee, Oliver handed Sky and Lennox new gear to replace what the water had destroyed or caused to malfunction. Lennox removed her old suit and pulled the new, dry Sparrow suit over her tights and undershirt and tied the laces tight on her new boots.

Oliver held out two discs. "Here, we only have a few working Kev discs left." Lennox and Sky activated them and they formed a thin layer of protection over their gray suits, sealing to their helmets.

Rain ceased to fall from the clouds, but the sky remained ominous. Lennox placed her hand over the Sparrow on her arm.

The time had come for her to fulfill her purpose. She and Oliver were finally going to finish what their parents started.

Finally....

Chapter 14

The clouds turned vicious shades of gray and purple. Easton occupied the passenger seat while Oliver sat in the driver's seat.

"Let's get moving before another storm comes," Easton said through the com system.

The two Sparrow Humvees rolled onto an old, muddy road. Easton turned to Sky and Lennox—who sat in the middle.

"We are Team One. Our priority is to activate the locket. Behind you are your Breachers." Easton pointed to a tall, lean man sitting in the back. "That's Hawk." She pointed to the other man who was smaller, but just as lean. "And Marshall."

The two men lifted up their hands, waving slightly.

"They'll get us in." She motioned to the large man sitting in the back with Hawk and Marshall. "And Tank will get us out."

Tank's dark lips exposed a bright white smile.

"Hello."

Lennox smiled back. "Nice to meet all of you."

Sky nodded and smiled with a wave.

Easton continued. "Team Two is behind us. They'll extract the prisoners from the stronghold."

Lennox looked out the back window and watched the remaining men load up.

"How far is the stronghold?" Sky asked.

"Two-hundred miles. We will get there in about three hours with our current route." Oliver answered.

Easton turned in her seat. "They're expecting an air attack, so we're coming at them from the ground. Once we are in, other Sparrow teams will bring in the stealth jets, ready to transport survivors and give air support should we need it. The plan is to take over the entire stronghold once we activate the locket. Keep an eye out for drones. The Regime has them out scouting the land."

"Got it." Sky stared out the window. His Sparrow uniform was stocked with tactical gear and he had strapped a new Striker over his shoulder, keeping it close.

Lennox traced the outline of the Sparrow over her

new tech suit and then squeezed her scarred arm. She narrowed her eyes and gripped the Striker that sat in her own lap. After their encounter with the tiny drones, she decided to keep her eyes open for anything off—small or big. Come what may, she would trust God to see her through. Her father spoke of a God-given purpose. She resolved to fulfill it. She believed in it.

The pair of Humvees rolled for miles. In the distance, smoke rose to the clouds.

"Over there." Lennox pointed to the thick gray smog.

Easton pulled out a hologram map. "It's a stronghold."

"What if there are Defiers there?" Sky leaned forward to Easton's seat. "Someone has to help them."

"It's about twenty miles out of the way." Easton looked at him.

"If we can help even one, isn't it worth it?" Sky persisted, his eyes serious.

Lennox anticipated Easton's response, looking between them. Their last discussion hadn't gone so well... or ended well, for that matter.

"We'll check it out." Easton placed the map on the

dashboard for Oliver.

"I'll let Team Two know the change of plans." Oliver pressed a button on the map, sending it to the other Humvee.

As they came closer to the rising smoke, Lennox's stomach twisted in knots. A Regime stronghold was burning down. The fenced prisoner's camp was ignited with bright orange flames. The Humvee rolled over the scattered remains of the town and then halted.

Stepping outside the vehicle, Easton signaled a few men to the west and others to the south. "Sky and Lennox, check the prisoner's camp. There might be survivors."

Lennox hoped so.

She and Sky crouched by a rounded opening in the chain-link fence. The pulse of electricity no longer ran through the metal and it looked as if someone had pried it from the ground to escape. They slid through the opening, stepping over the crumbled cement and shredded children's toys that covered the dirt. How many lost their lives here? How many children?

A man's silhouette lay in the dust. Lennox ran toward him and removed the rubble that rested on top of him. Sky crouched beside her. She placed two fingers on the fallen man's neck. She shook her head and Sky sighed. The man's body was cold and his soul already gone. She closed his sunken brown eyes. Sky patted Lennox on the shoulder.

"We better keep moving. I'll check over there." He made his way toward a building with a ditch beside it.

Lennox swallowed hard. "Okay."

The other side of the fence held strong memories for Lennox. She was held in a place much like this not too long ago, digging a ditch just like the one Sky walked toward. A gust of wind swirled up dust, making it hard to see. The fire crackled.

"Help!" a child cried.

Lennox squinted through the dust and blaze, searching for where the cry came from. Lennox ran over pockets of fire with long strides to find the voice. The smoke was thick and she struggled to see.

"Call out!" Lennox pleaded as she spun around, searching.

"Over here!" the young voice scratched.

A little boy around the age of ten had his arms wrapped around something protectively. Lennox

141

thought it was a stuffed doll at first, but then realized it was a little girl around three years old. She had dark brown ringlets that surrounded her chubby baby cheeks. Lennox steadily ran closer. The boy looked up at Lennox and screamed.

"Watch out!"

A form approached. She saw the glint of metal.

Gun!

Lennox flung over the children to shield their bodies with her tech suit. A flood of bullets flew straight toward her back and she hoped it would not malfunction. She felt the first round pound into her spine, and then another. She grit her teeth and waited for the next bullet to pummel the tech. She squeezed the little boy tighter and felt his shallow breaths. He and the little girl had been inhaling the black smoke longer than her. She had no idea how they had not passed out yet. Another shot fired. The bullet missed her suit. She turned her head and saw the man fall to the ground, wincing. To the man's right, Sky aimed his firearm at their enemy. He walked to where she and the children were.

"Are you guys okay?"

Sky bent down and unwrapped Lennox's shivering arms. All Lennox could do was nod, "Yes."

Sky reached out to the boy and tried to unwrap his arms from around the little girl, but he was immovable. The little girl trembled with eyes shut tight, refusing to look at anyone.

"It's okay, you're okay now." Lennox slowly unhinged the little boy's hands from around the girl. "Is this your sister?" she asked.

The boy nodded.

"You were really brave to protect her like that." She wiped soot from his face. His clothes were darkened by residual smoke.

"My father told me to protect her." He wiped small tears that built up in his deep brown eyes.

"And you did a very good job at that. What's your name?" Lennox asked.

"I'm James." He spread the tears around his face with the back of his hands.

"Hi, James. I'm Lennox. We are going to get you and your sister to safety, okay?" Lennox reached out to grab hold of one of his hands.

"Okay." James let Lennox hold his left hand.

"What's your sister's name?" Lennox asked, watching the little girl cling to James' shirt with one hand as she sucked her thumb with the other.

"Annabeth."

"Hi, Annabeth." Lennox knelt beside her while still holding James' hand. "I'm Lennox, and this is Sky. We are going to help you and your brother."

Annabeth's tears rolled down both of her cheeks, streaking the black soot on her face. Lennox held out her free arm and waited for the little girl to wrap her chubby arms around her neck before standing. Annabeth wrapped her legs around Lennox's waist and buried her face in Lennox's neck. Sky took James by the other hand and led him over the burning debris.

Walking around the torn down razor-wire fence, Sky looked at Lennox and shook his head. "Unbelievable."

The Regime had bombed the entire stronghold, not just the prison.

Ahab had turned on even his own.

Chapter 15

"We can't take them with us." Easton stood in front of the two rescued children. They clung together with tear-stained faces nestled close. She folded her arms. "It's too dangerous. There's a secluded defiant city not far from here we can take them to."

"There are surviving defiant cities?" Lennox asked.

"Yes, all over the world. Defiers are fighting back. They'll keep the children safe." Easton turned to the Humvee. "We will take them there together. Team Two, load up. Annabeth and James can ride with us."

Lennox stooped low to look into their faces. She took Annabeth and James by their hands.

"Come on, we're going take you some place safe. I bet both of you are hungry."

She took them to the Humvee and let James in first. Then she picked Annabeth up and sat her gently by Sky, who had already opened two MREs for them.

"Here, these will fill you up." Sky held out the two packages. "Go on, it's okay. They're meatloaf and gravy. One of my favorites, actually."

James took them quickly and handed one to his sister. They wasted no time and took their first bites. They were starving.

Lennox sat beside Annabeth and watched the little girl scarf down the food. How long had it been since they ate a real meal? It must be awful to be so young and not understand the reasons for your suffering.

"Roll out" Oliver said, putting the Humvee in gear and driving forward.

They drove past abandoned cities and burned farmland. Every sign of life was obliterated—not even animals roamed the desolate wasteland as they crossed.

After miles on off roads, Easton said, "This is it."

Oliver stopped the vehicle. "Are you sure?" He glanced around. "There's nothing here."

"I'm sure." Easton opened her door and stepped onto the cracked earth.

Nothing resembled human life. No movement. No noise. No one. A slow wind moved through the open barren land.

Over twenty men stepped out from behind what few dead trees remained with their rifles aimed at the Humvees. Lennox saw movement out of the corner of her eye and saw more camouflaged men hiding. Her chest tightened. They didn't look friendly.

Easton raised her hands in the air with her Striker secured on her back. "We're Sparrows. We rescued two children and are only seeking protection for them."

Annabeth cried, and Lennox pulled her close. James reached for Sky's hand. Sky took it and smiled.

"Everything's going to be okay, buddy."

A man who towered over six-feet tall walked closer to the Humvees. He held his right fist up to signal the others. They stopped, angling weapons downward. Lennox held tighter to Annabeth.

"Sparrows, huh? We've heard that one before. Have all your men exit the vehicles."

Easton nodded. "Everyone out."

Lennox slowly stepped out, keeping Annabeth close. She kept her weapon strapped over her shoulder. Sky did the same and kept James near. When the man saw the children, his eyes softened.

"We found them twenty miles away at an

abolished stronghold." Easton reached out to shake the man's hand. "I'm Easton."

He accepted the gesture and offered two firm shakes. "Jack."

Jack raised two fingers to his lips and whistled loud. Men came out from their positions.

"Welcome to Hope."

He led them through the trees and around winding paths before they arrived at the city called Hope. Women and children gardened while men worked on houses. The atmosphere was filled with sounds of joy. It was good to hear laughter. It was good to see life. Lennox squeezed Annabeth's hand.

"How do you keep the Regime from finding this place?" Oliver questioned.

"Pray. I believe God has kept us hidden from their drones. There's really no other way to explain it. We should've been wiped off the map already. They get close… *real close*… but here we still are."

"What about the storms caused by the GWS?" Oliver peered at the cloudy sky.

"Storm cellars. We get pretty bad tornadoes that creep near here, but they haven't hit us directly, yet."

Jack extended his strong hands to greet a little girl about the age of six. She had shoulder-length auburn ringlets that bobbed with her every movement.

She jumped into his arms. "Daddy!" The sundress she wore floated in the air as Jack placed her little feet back onto the soil.

"My daughter, Sarah."

The little girl waved and stepped closer to Annabeth. "Hiya," she said softly. "Do you want to play?"

Annabeth looked up to Lennox, who smiled and nodded as she released the rescued child's chubby hand. Annabeth stuck out her bottom lip and shook her head. Lennox knelt down and hugged her tight.

"It's safer here." Lennox smiled. "You'll have food and friends to play with. Trust me, you'll like it here."

Annabeth sucked her bottom lip back in. "Otay." She rubbed her forearm across her nose, but before Sarah could pull Annabeth away, she reached for her brother to tag along. He let Sarah and his sister drag him to a small playground with swings and a slide.

It was strange—yet nice to see such an act of

innocence amidst such despair. The children reminded Lennox of Clover.

"So you'll keep them safe?" Lennox asked Jack. She was already attached to them and wanted nothing more than to keep them happy.

"As if they were my own." Jack waved at his giggling daughter. "I assume you all are on a mission."

"Yes, sir." Oliver stepped closer.

"You have my prayers." Jack shook Oliver's hand.

"Thank you, sir." Oliver patted Jack's shoulder.

"I'm sorry, but we have to leave *now*," Easton urged. "There are reports of storms in the south that we have to beat."

"I understand," Jack said. "My wife and I will keep them safe. I promise."

Easton nodded. "Here." She held out a hologram message portal. "It will directly link you to Sparrow City. Call us whenever you need to. We're in this together."

"Thank you, I will." Jack put the small device in the front pocket of his red plaid shirt. "God be with you."

"And with you." Easton walked back to where they

entered the city. "Sparrows, it's time."

Walking back to the Humvees, a dozen of Jack's men escorted them through the trees and stopped at the clearing where the Humvees sat. Lennox waved goodbye and sat back at her place, holding her Striker with sweaty palms.

The Sparrows drove straight into the stormy darkness.

Chapter 16

Dark funnel clouds threatened to touch the earth. Lennox admired their beauty and quivered at their potential.

Oliver drove faster on the forsaken highway. His jaw was so tight it caused the tendons in his face to show. The dust on the side of the road swirled as gusts of wind pushed against the Humvee. Clumps of rocks spun up into the wheels, adding to the ferocious sound of nature.

The funnel clouds gave in to the gravitational pull of earth and shaped into dangerous twin tornadoes. They touched the ground with such force that the vehicle vibrated beneath the team. Both tornadoes headed straight toward them and started to suck the vehicle into their vortex.

"Floor it!" Easton shouted.

"I am!" Oliver set the Humvee in reverse and whipped it around, setting it back in drive. Trees leaned

152

back and started to uproot, surrendering to the tornadoes' pull.

"They're too close!" Lennox shouted over the winds that howled like a lone wolf searching for his pack. The sound made the hair on the back of her neck rise. Debris spun in circles all around them. Full grown trees twisted in the air as if they weighed nothing.

The noise. Lennox would never forget the sound of the world turning against itself. Watching a tornado on the live-feed at Sparrow City did not do the beast justice.

"Right! Turn right!" Easton shouted, looking at the hologram map. There's an underground parking lot at an abandoned mall." Easton traced her pointer finger along the route and held on to the dashboard as the ride got bumpier. "We can wait it out there."

Lennox braced herself against the Humvee's inner frame as Oliver turned right, driving over curbs and rubble. With every bounce, Lennox's body shot skyward and then harshly sat back in place. The tornadoes seemed to track them like evil twins on a desperate mission to see who could kill first.

Oliver steered the Humvee closer to the abandoned

lot with Team Two close behind. The tornadoes were now less than a football field away. Rolling into the underground structure, the cement pillars looked as if they would give way any minute as the tornadoes rampaged closer. Dust spurted out of them with every slight shift of the building.

Lennox saw the destruction that occurred through the slanted entrance they used. The tornadoes lingered just outside until they joined together, forming one massive catastrophe. The mega-beast plucked up street signs and lamp posts, devouring them whole.

Teams One and Two waited... and waited.

Lennox clung to the inner frame of the shaking Humvee as the tornado powerfully shook the concrete foundation. She had never seen such a vicious tornado in the flesh and she questioned what would be left when it was over. She and her family always waited out storms in their storm cellar. She had only witnessed their aftermath.

One minute turned into ten. Fifteen. Twenty.

How long was the storm going to be? Normal tornadoes lasted less than thirty minutes... usually. Then again, this was no normal tornado. It was a man-made terror meant to wipe out entire civilizations.

The deafening howls of wind sent chills up Lennox's spine. Her nails dug into the interior of the vehicle. Through the howls, she made out the noise of twisting metal screeching against pavement.

Lennox remembered Oliver's words. "When the darkness seems closer than the light, pray." Lennox bowed her head and closed her eyes.

"Lord, calm the storm for us." If anyone could calm the storm, God could. With all sincerity, she leaned her head against the window of the vehicle and expectantly waited.

Sky touched Lennox's knee, resting his hand there. "It's going to be okay." His face showed signs of worry, though he would never admit it.

Lennox took her eyes away from the storm, nodded, and softened her grip against the metal frame. She rested her hand on top of Sky's, which remained on her knee. The Humvee trembled and dust exploded from the pillars. She clutched tighter to Sky's hand. He entwined his fingers with hers.

Was it going to be okay?

The winds cried louder as broken pieces of the

shattered world were whisked higher and deeper into the storm. Louder. She could not hear anything except the chaos outside. She rested her head against the window again and breathed steadily—in through her nose, out through her mouth. Then...

Silence.

Complete and utter nothingness.

Was it over?

Lennox glanced at Sky. It was too quiet—as if no one breathed and nothing moved.

He smiled. "See, nothing to worry about."

Oliver turned around. "Everyone okay?"

Calm. The back row of Sparrows gave a thumbs-up and Lennox and Sky nodded.

Suddenly, blasts of cement sputtered out from the wall and the earth trembled. The howling screams returned. Leaves and twigs whipped through the parking garage's entrance.

Lennox inhaled and held on to the Humvee's door and Sky's hand with white knuckles. The ground shook more violently than before. She grit her teeth and curled her toes inside her boots as the roar grew louder. Everything shook. Her body hit the side and then shoved into Sky's. She had never experienced anything like this. Was an earthquake answering the tornado's call? The earth could not hold itself together.

Sky gently covered Lennox's body with his own as the vehicle bounced. Easton and Oliver yelled. Lennox only heard the muffled roars of the organic beast.

And then, silence. *Again.*

The quaking ceased and the earth's cries dissolved within itself. Outside, a sliver of sunshine peeked through. The death clouds returned to the heavens right in front of them as gracious light fully reemerged.

Lennox let out a sigh of relief. "Thank you, God!" It could have been so much worse. For now, the storm was over.

Oliver rolled the Humvee out of the abandoned garage. They survived, though not much else had. The tornado had torn through a mere twenty feet from where they were. Smooth cement was turned to piles of jagged stone and utility poles lay broke in half. Lennox shook her head. She hoped the town had been long abandoned by its residents.

The Global Weather Simulator was out of control. No one knew where it would strike next. That "next time" might be in a populated area. Lennox imagined how the war would change once she successfully utilized her father's hard work. No GWS meant one less source of power for the Regime.

The ride smoothed out when they reached the unbroken road. The Sparrows in back looked left and right, up and down. Vigilance was required. They couldn't afford any more setbacks, now.

Lennox kept her eyes tuned for any sign of tracking drones. She also watched the clouds with the anticipation that another storm could break out.

Sometimes life took you through one storm, only to put you in a bigger one.

Chapter 17

Six miles away from the Regime stronghold, a figure stood in the shadows ahead of the Sparrow convoy. Looking out the Humvee's window, Lennox recognized the figure's all too familiar glowing yellow eyes.

A Prowler.

Oliver swerved around the predator. Tank opened the back window and aimed his weapon. With one shot, the Prowler illuminated blue with Sparrow serum before he could take hold of anyone's mind.

Team Two's Humvee veered off the path. The driver swerved, trying to avoid a collision with the trees, but the vehicle deviated too far and ran over something fatal. It went up in flames.

No!

They were in a minefield.

The fire whipped against the clouds and trees as the vehicle flew through the air. Lennox thought of the men inside the burning Humvee. She wrestled with her emotions. She watched the Humvee crash to the ground and hoped the suits could protect them. She waited to see if Team Two would emerge from the wreckage. They didn't. Team Two was gone.

Gone.

It hurt to think about. Hurt to breathe. Her heart ached inside her chest, pounding away at her ribcage.

A multitude of glowing eyes encompassed them. Oliver veered the Humvee to the right, but Prowlers were in the trees and behind the brush. He spun the wheel with nowhere to go. To the left there was a minefield. To the right, a new breed of Prowlers surrounded them like killer bees whose hive had been disturbed.

Team One was in the middle of the hive. She could not even number them before they swarmed closer. Lennox thought back to when she was a little girl and how her mother cleansed her childhood bedroom of the "monsters" that hid behind walls and in closets by quoting Psalm 23:4. "Even though I walk through the darkest valley, I will fear no evil, for you are with me."

God, I know you are with us. I will fear no evil.

Help us.

Her battle for faith raged as the Prowlers tried to grab hold of her mind. Easton, Oliver, and Sky shook their heads and scrunched their faces as they fought too.

A wicked war machine rolled into view. The black metal giant was shaped like a scorpion with a segmented, curved tail. As the tail unfurled, the machine positioned itself to fire an innumerable amount of fiery barbs that resembled spears.

Lennox clenched her jaw and steadied her gun, aiming out of the window. She fired a round. Sky did the same on his side. The bullets were useless against the scorpion shaped machine. Easton dropped five Prowlers before they could grab hold of the Sparrows' minds. How much longer could they fend them off?

Adrenaline kept Lennox's mind and actions from straying too far, allowing her to compartmentalize everything. She positioned her gun, aiming at a Prowler.

Hit!

She closed her eyes for a brief second. "Phew." One down, a dozen more to go. The Regime advanced closer and closer. Escape couldn't come fast enough.

Oliver spun the wheel too quickly, losing control. Lennox was weightless as her team's Humvee spun. She watched the war machine turn upside down as her body bounced inside the Humvee.

Smash.

The vehicle landed hard on the muddy ground, leaving Lennox in a ball inside and Oliver and Easton dangling from their seatbelts. Lennox stared in a fuzzy daze. Oliver fumbled with his seatbelt.

"Easton! Lennox!"

She vaguely registered her brother's screams. Her body lay on the crumpled roof. The nanotubes of her suit took the brunt of the blows, keeping her body whole. She caught her breath and unfolded her body from the fetal position. She looked to her left. Sky managed to wiggle out of the wreckage. He helped release Oliver.

"You help Easton, I got Lennox."

Lennox looked at Tank, Haiden, and Marshall, who already fired their weapons to keep the monsters at bay. Sky lay on his stomach, coming into Lennox's view. He reached to her from outside the Humvee.

162

"Lennox, you have to get out. They're coming. Come on, I'll help you." Sky rushed her.

Move, Lennox, MOVE.

Her body wouldn't listen. The Regime barged toward them. Prowlers crept closer. The scorpion machine dominated the environment. Emblazoned barbs landed all around them.

MOVE!

A rush of energy swept through her and she reached her hand toward Sky. He pulled her out of the bent window frame.

Lennox noticed the blood that spilled from his brow. "Your helmet and Kev tech. It's not working."

"It's okay, let's get you to safety." Sky waved his hand in rebuttal.

It's not okay.

The gash on his head split open too wide. There was too much bright red blood. Lennox had seen too many Sparrow training videos to *not* be concerned.

Oliver yelled, "Sky, over here!"

Easton and Oliver fired their weapons, hiding themselves behind the overturned Humvee. Both rested their backs against the flipped metal frame and rose to fire simultaneously every few seconds. Regime soldiers fell to the ground with their veins glowing blue.

"Come on, they'll cover us." Sky stayed in front of Lennox, standing between her and the line of fire. The protector—always the protector.

Lennox held her weapon up to the right, firing as the Prowlers charged forward. She had to keep them out of their minds—but with every Prowler she shot, another took its place. There were too many! Team One was outnumbered and outmanned.

Loud shots fired, ringing in Lennox's ears. She crouched lower as she followed Sky. His movements were precise and swift, but he slowed before they made it to Oliver and Easton.

His body fell. Blood pooled around him. He looked like a stone statue lying in the dirt.

No. God, please, NO!

Lennox fell to her knees beside her bleeding friend. She should have made him stay behind her. She knew his suit had malfunctioned. She took off her helmet that fired digital warnings across her visor.

CRITICAL... CRITICAL... CRITICAL...

The light in Sky's eyes weakened.

"Sky, we're going to get you help. Stay with me." She held her hand over the gushing blood that poured from his torso. She watched his face dim and eyes fade. His eyelids drifted closed. "No, Sky, stay with me. You hear me? In Jesus' name, you shall live and not die." Lennox tapped his cheek. His eyes fluttered. "Sky, you have to stay awake, okay? Just stay awake. Keep your eyes on me. I got you. I got you." Lennox said as she held her hands in place over the bullet wound and sucked back panic.

Assess, stabilize, move. You can do this, come on! Come on, Sky. Come on. Stay with me. Please! You have to.

Lennox looked over her shoulder. She couldn't see or hear Oliver and Easton anymore. Where did they go? They wouldn't leave her or Sky.

Something was wrong. She felt it in the marrow of her bones.

As Lennox turned back around, her face met the butt of a rifle.

Chapter 18

Lennox regained consciousness with a pounding headache. Her nose was swollen and bloody, and her hazy vision revealed blurry tree branches with swaying leaves. She lay flat on her back. She watched leaves float down peacefully to her side. It would have been beautiful—even tranquil—if not for the circumstance.

She blinked hard to regain her bearings and tried to sit up. Her breath left fog swirling in the now frigid air, but she didn't feel cold. Her hands and feet were zip-tied. She fought against the ties that bound her, but they weren't ordinary zip-ties.

"Ouch!" The bands were electrified and burned her skin every time she fought against them.

Her brain cleared.

Sky.

She squirmed to free herself despite the shocking pain. A burly Regime soldier grabbed hold of her zip-tied ankles and dragged her over the leaf-covered ground. Her shoulders plowed through the foliage and left a clear trail of dirt in her wake. She tried to kick free, but her efforts were of no use. He pulled her with ease as if she were a sack of bones. She would have to outsmart him... fast.

To her right, she saw Sky's bloody body being pulled in the same manner. "You're lucky I recognized you before one of my guys killed you," the man said, dragging her further into the woods without looking at her. The veins in his hands bulged.

"What?" Lennox held her head off the ground to avoid being bludgeoned to death by the rocks he pulled her over.

Oh, God, did they kill Easton...Oliver?

Where's Oliver?

Lennox's eyes released the hurt forming in her heart. She refused to believe they were gone. They couldn't be. God got them out somehow... someway... and they would come for her. Oliver would come for her.

The man peered over his shoulder at Lennox. "Your reputation precedes you, Lennox Winters. Ahab has pictures of you everywhere on tech screens, hologram portals, and newsfeeds. You're quite famous, or should I say, *infamous*." He let out a slow husky laugh. "There is a huge bounty for you. You'll feed me and my men for weeks."

Money was all the motivation some men needed to do the unspeakable.

"Does he want me dead or alive?" Lennox asked.

"He wants you alive." The man tugged harder and walked faster to his destination.

It would be so much easier if he didn't. Lennox assumed Ahab would torture her. She couldn't fathom what else he had in store. She knew she'd be dead already if Ahab didn't need her alive for something. Perhaps he planned on making an example of her like he did with the family and the flag. Hadn't he already tried that route and failed? Maybe he wanted another stab at it.

Up above the trees there was a chirp, and then a song. Lennox zeroed in on a red sparrow that flew along her sightline.

God is with me.

In the darkness, she reached out to hope… to light.

Lord, I trust You.

168

One of the most important statements Lennox would ever make... to trust Him. That phrase said it all. With three little words she declared everything she needed to in one moment.

She thought of the picture Sky drew her, and the verse. She was stronger than Ahab knew. God had delivered her before and He was faithful to deliver them all again. She just had to trust God fully and not let what was happening outside determine her faith on the inside. Faith was never about what was seen, it was about the unseen. Lennox reminded herself of that as they drug her and Sky through the wilderness.

What can mere men do to us?

The Regime soldiers stripped Lennox of her jumpsuit and boots, but allowed her to wear her undershirt and leggings. A soldier threw her into a hole where it was cold and dark and her body hit the ground hard. Praise God she didn't break any bones on the way down.

She looked ten feet up. The only entrance or exit was the bars above her—too high to reach, but low enough to tease her. The rest of her new prison was made of stone and dirt.

Had Defiers dug this pit? She thought back to the hole she dug while imprisoned at her first stronghold.

This hole smelled of wet earth and rotting flesh. Lennox gagged at the scent.

At least, the zip-ties are gone.

Lennox sighed as her eyes adjusted to her dingy surroundings. She looked around and hollered out.

"Sky! Sky!"

She hoped their captors placed him close by but he was nowhere to be seen or heard. She was the only one inside the pit, screaming his name to herself. She sat down in the center of her prison and closed her eyes, resting her head on her knees with her arms wrapped around her legs. She would wait patiently for the Lord.

Couldn't the Regime think of anything new? She had already been through this once before and could do it again. She was much stronger than the girl she used to be, and that girl was pretty strong. She was a survivor, a fighter.

"When I'm afraid, I will trust God." *Just trust, Lennox. He'll get us through this too.*

As she interceded for Sky, Oliver, and her team, her body gave way to sleep. Nightmares chased her faith as she tossed and turned on the hard, cold ground. Lennox choked on cold water.

Was she dreaming?

Her eyes shot open and she turned her head to cough. Black boots shifted in the mud the water had created. A soldier stood before Lennox with a bucket in his hands.

She sat straight up and breathed in the air around her, hard and fast. She wiped her face off and saw the Regime soldier hover over her with a smirk on his face. She weighed her options.

She could lunge at him, press his back against the wall and wrestle his gun away from him, or she could pretend to pass out and then go for his gun when he checked on her. Her third choice was to obey.

Another soldier stood guard above them with his gun pointed straight at her. She lost her options and stared at the soldier who held the gun without blinking. Anger boiled within her.

"Get up! Ahab wants to see you," the soldier with narrowed dark eyes said.

Of course he does.

Lennox took too long and the soldier yanked her up by the arm.

"I heard you have a listening problem," he said through gritted teeth.

He took Lennox by the elbow and pointed to the ladder. The soldier at the top continued to point the rapid-fire weapon at her while the other prodded her with his gun from down below. She took the first rung and then the next until she reached the top.

The sun was bright and hot. Its light burned her retinas. She placed her forearm over her eyes as a shield. Sweat dripped from her forehead. Wasn't it just cold in the woods? Everything seemed like déjà vu. She shook her head. The soldier's gun pressed hard in the small of her back.

"Move!"

Lennox obeyed and walked to the nearest building like a lamb led to slaughter. She stood before a high-rise that was at least seventy-five stories tall.

This stronghold was more city-like than any other. The skyline was beautiful with similar glass buildings that towered right next to each other—very different from the Texas she knew. Her Texas consisted of farmland and small-town charm. She had only visited big cities with high-rises.

The Regime stronghold had no charm, but rather a distinct, icy, disconnected feeling where only power mattered. There had to be insiders—traitors— everywhere. How else could the Regime evolve so quickly? The stronghold reminded Lennox of a highly advanced civilization that tested bombs on itself. Some buildings were being built while others were showered with bullet holes from a firefight. There was no telling how much time this stronghold had to prepare for Ahab's appearance.

As the soldiers led her to the doors, the mirrored glass reflected Lennox's rundown appearance. Dirt and bruises covered her from being thrown in the pit. Her body may look pitiful, but what the soldier couldn't see was the roar of a lion inside. It would come out at the right time.

Sliding glass doors opened and the soldier nudged Lennox in.

"Have a seat," said a lady in a nice red business dress. She was dolled up with makeup and her hair was fashioned in a fancy bun on the side.

The woman seemed out of place to Lennox. Didn't she know this was a war zone—that people were being slaughtered right outside the pretty sliding glass doors?

Lennox took a seat on a clear acrylic chair. It was much like the acrylic Prowler cage she shattered with her praise months ago. It made her smile a little and boosted her faith. It was good to be reminded of how far God had brought her by something as simple as a clear chair. She saw God in everything now. He worked on her heart in the pit. Even through the nightmares, God kept her through the darkest of nights.

Regime soldiers stood at attention by the sliding glass doors and a dozen more stood around the building with guns clenched in their hands. Their eyes lingered on Lennox's every move. It gave her a sense of joy to observe how they anticipated her making a move—she would not disappoint them. With God's help, she would overcome them.

Lennox waited until the minutes turned into hours. The sun disappeared and the moon rose by the time the fancy woman in the business dress came back to get Lennox.

"This way, Miss Winters." The lady motioned her hand like an airplane attendant.

How nice of the woman to sort of act civilized toward the prisoners.

Lennox thought of all the sarcastic comments she could make, but refrained as she followed her tour guide down hallway after hallway.

She heard screams of torment and looked on horrifically at what she saw through the room's windows. Men and women in lab coats tapped on syringes of yellow liquid. A man was strapped down to a table with wild eyes and foam coming from his mouth.

Lennox was hit... hard. She realized what this place was.

They made Prowlers here.

Chapter 19

They're going to try to make me a Prowler.

Her heart raced and her mouth was dry. Ahab wanted to turn her in to one of his dreadful, mindless monsters. Out of all the possibilities she suspected, this was not one of them. Perhaps she should have. If they could stop her they could prevent the Sparrows from using the locket. Did Ahab know that? He had to know something. He always seemed one step ahead in the game and would stop at nothing to destroy what Lennox represented: faith, purpose, and hope.

Walking through the doorway to the room, she was guided to a bed table that confirmed her suspicions. It was cold. The smell of chemicals burned her throat. Everything was white under the bright florescent lights that shined above.

Lennox fought against the two soldiers as they strapped her to the upright laboratory table. She head-butted one of them, sending him flailing backward. The lady casually inserted a needle into her neck.

"That's enough of that." She pushed the syringe's liquid into Lennox's bloodstream.

Lennox's body felt heavy as every muscle gave way. If it weren't for the straps holding her against the slanted medical table, she would have fallen face first onto the white marble floor.

"Ahab will be with you shortly." The lady left and the soldiers took their position outside of the "Room of White."

Lennox could barely hold her head up, so she rested it on the back of the table. Her vision blurred and the vertigo would not leave. The white straps that held her were tight and dug into her skin. It was awkward to lay limp and still be held as if standing at an angle.

The lab reminded Lennox of an insane asylum, which was not a place she wanted to be at all.

The room spun when Ahab entered and she was not sure if it was really him. He still wore his impeccable suit and shoes, but the skin on his face did not seem as tight. He looked as if he had lost a lot of weight. He wasn't very big to begin with, but now his eyes were gaunt and his skin was patched with red. The

Commander of the Regime appeared frail—as if at death's door.

Ahab glowered as she struggled to comprehend what she saw.

"That locket I got from you did this to me," Ahab's voice sounded like a fork that scraped against a dinner plate. She hated it.

Her father must have installed a chemical agent to keep anyone who wasn't supposed to open the locket at bay. Could tech possibly read a person's motivation like that? Lennox considered that maybe the locket wasn't doing this to Ahab after all. Maybe it was the wrath of God, much like the wrath Pharaoh felt during the plagues in Moses' day when he would not let God's people go. Wasn't Ahab doing the same thing Pharaoh once did?

One thing Lennox did know was that you don't mess with the people of the one true living God. It never worked in anyone's favor even if it looked like it would for a moment. One day, Ahab would give an account for his evil deeds on why he slaughtered all those innocent people—the women and the children. He would answer for their bloodshed—whether now or later—one day, he *would* answer.

Lennox bit her tongue, coaxing it into submission so she would remain silent as if deaf and mute. The tongue was the most unruly member of the body and if she could keep it in control, she could stay in control. Sparrow training taught her to not speak during interrogations, unless absolutely necessary. She never thought she would need to use this type of training so soon. She never expected to be like this before Ahab, again.

She stared straight through him with defiance. She wished she could voice her anger and hurl judgment upon him.

Not yet.

She resolved to remain silent, as she was taught.

"So that's how you're going to play it? Good." Ahab twisted his pasty hands together and flakes of dead skin fell to the ground. He was worse off than Lennox first thought. "More reason for me to hurt the ones you love."

"No!"

Ahab had Sky!

Lennox squirmed, her muscles slowly coming back

to life. She could not free herself even the slightest. The restraints were too strong and her muscles were too weak. She had to figure out how to get both of them out before it was too late.

"I thought you were smarter," Ahab continued. "I guess I have given you too much credit. You're weak. How could they have ever thought you were strong enough to retrieve the locket? Your fellow Sparrows have put too much trust in you. You *are* nothing... nothing more than a pest in a field." He let the words linger on his tongue. "A mere speck in the scheme of what is about to come."

Lennox disagreed. She knew God had a plan and purpose for her life, but Ahab's words still stabbed violently at her. Her exact fears were displayed by his audible words. She *had* let the other Sparrows down, just as she had let the Defiers down. They were in prison, waiting for a miracle. They depended on her to change everything. Right now, she felt like she could change nothing. She was nothing...

Lennox wanted to scream, to say something... anything to find and help Sky. Fighting the resistance against her wrists and ankles, she let out the question that lingered in the front of her mind. "Where's Sky?"

"I'm so glad you asked! He is... well... let's just say he is processing."

"Pro... cess... ing?" The word was hard for Lennox to get out. Her voice scratched. It hurt to speak.

"Yes, he will make an excellent addition to my collection of Prowlers. He didn't even really put up that much of a fight. I guess the anger from his grandfather's death gave us the perfect avenue to access his dark side."

Lennox knew that Sky was not grieving healthily. She saw it in his eyes and felt it in his words. He gave in to vengeance and wrath—vengeance that did not belong to him and wrath that would only destroy him.

"Please, don't do this." Lennox wished her arms were free to strangle the stupid, usual grin off Ahab's face.

She thought of the stranger she saw on the laboratory table with foam coming out of his mouth. Was that how Sky looked like now? Eyes wild... inhuman... Prowler?

"It's already done." Ahab left the room. The door crept shut behind him.

Chapter 20

It's already done.

The sentence played on a loop in her ears. A rush of heat came over her body as panic set in. Her heart thumped hard against her chest.

She stayed in the white room—a terrible prison where all she had were her thoughts, blank walls, and the screams from other rooms and halls. She listened carefully for Sky's scream, but it never came. If only she could hear his voice and know that he was okay. She knew he wasn't, but she dreamed he was.

The door opened. The same woman who injected her with the sedative was back with another dose. Lennox noticed the embroidery on the upper left side of her nice dress. It was the Regime's emblem of a snake coiled around letters that formed a name—Simmons.

The woman named Simmons tilted her head and curved her lips down into a frown. "We can't have you squirming around in here. You'll hurt yourself."

How kind of her to care.

Lennox forced strength to her voice. "Why are you doing this? Why would you ever work for a man who makes people monsters?"

"Oh dear, they're not monsters. The Prowlers are highly evolved, genetically advanced specimens of human perfection."

"I'm not talking about the Prowlers."

Lennox's eyes were wide as she wrestled with the restraints. This terrible woman was just as much of a monster as the Prowler, if not more so. She had no venom running in her veins. She was a monster without it.

Simmons raised a perfectly arched eyebrow. "You're clever, aren't you?" She paused and breathed in heavily. "I'm no monster. I'm a survivor." Her ivory skin creased in her forehead as her eyebrows raised higher.

"You survive by cowardice." Lennox tried to swallow after taking in the air when she spoke. It only made her mouth feel like it was stuffed with cotton balls. She would not give an inch, even if it did hurt to speak.

The woman smiled her perfect, straight smile. Her teeth were bright white, her red lipstick matched her snarky attitude.

"Ah, yes, you're righteous and I'm a coward. I much rather be a coward where I am than righteous where you are." She stuck the needle in Lennox's neck and pushed the medicine into her veins. She curved her strawberry lips into a wicked smile.

Lennox's strength gave way to the sedation. This time, she could not even pick up her head. It dangled like a carrot from a stick. Not even her tongue could move. The medicine must have been altered to a greater dose.

"That's better, isn't it?" the woman whispered to herself, taking a strap and putting it over Lennox's forehead and connecting it to the back of the bed. "There. Now you won't have any problems seeing your next guest."

Next guest?

Lennox's heart hurt from the constant, heavy thumps in her chest. She heard the rhythm of her heartbeat in her ears as it pounded against her skull. It was the one muscle that continued to fight back against the medicine. Her mind fired warnings.

Ahab strolled into the room with two guards.

"You're looking rather peaked, Lennox. I must tell them to lower your dosage." Ahab smiled cruelly. "I have good news, Sky is doing marvelously. Better than expected, really. I think he is some of our finest work."

In her mind, Lennox moved and fought to escape. Every part of her screamed out, reaching out to be free.

One of the guards rolled in an old music player. Lennox guessed it had to be from the early nineteen hundreds. It definitely wasn't something she saw recently. It had a large metal horn-like attachment where the sound came out. Lennox remembered Sky's Pop having one similar in the attic. What was it called? A *phonograph.* What would Ahab want a phonograph for? It belonged in a museum, not in the updated building that consisted of science labs and white asylum rooms.

Ahab placed a black disc on top and moved the arm with the needle over it. Music played, but it was not music to Lennox's ears. It was the Anthem of the Regime. It echoed off the white walls and into Lennox's eardrums, stabbing away at her fortitude. The same Anthem played outside on the building's broadcasting system. Lennox heard it mix with the noise coming from the phonograph.

The two guards raised their right fists against their hearts in recognition of the blasting music. Lennox visualized all the people outside who bowed to the crooked man that was Ahab. She wondered how could they be so deceived.

"You hear that, Lennox? That's the sound of victory." Ahab twisted his flakey hands together in triumph.

The only way Lennox could show her displeasure was with sweaty palms and the tears that ran down her cheeks.

A man in a white lab coat entered the room. He bowed down on one knee and then stood to whisper something into Ahab's ear.

"Excellent! Bring him in." Ahab clapped, overjoyed.

Adrenaline rushed through Lennox.

Sky stood in the doorway.

What have they done to you?

His wild eyes scanned her. Nothing seemed to

register with him. Did he not recognize her? His lack of emotion made it clear that he did not recognize her at all.

Her heart pounded faster at the sight of what he had become.

NO!

She screamed from the depths of her soul, yet her agony never reached her lips. The medicine seeping through her veins made her deepest pleas mild and non-existent. It couldn't happen this way! Not Sky, not *her* Sky.

"What'd you do to him?" Lennox's voice found a way out, but it was too soft to show her true rage—an inferno exploded within her.

"Well, I *saved* his life." Ahab twisted his hands and tilted his head to the left. "You're welcome." He got closer and laughed uncontrollably, breathing into her face. "You ought to show a little gratitude."

Ahab waved his hand in the air.

Sky walked farther into the room, wearing the same fatigues with the emblem of a snake coiled on the sleeve as the men that murdered her parents. His skin was tinged with a light yellow and his eyes were wild… glowing. He stood right in front of her—inhuman—yet still Sky. He did not look as animalistic as the older, "outdated" Prowlers. His face remained handsome and his body statuesque. He was the upgrade—the genetically "modified to perfection," stronger, faster, and tamer version that was easier for Ahab to manipulate.

Sky stood next to Ahab without a twitch, ready for a command—just as a dog would sit by his master.

Lennox was sick to her stomach. If she could, she would throw up the acid in her throat.

Sky raised his right fist to his heart and then lowered it back down by his side. Lennox closed her eyes and prayed to God.

This could not be happening. She needed Sky. She couldn't lose him. She had lost too much. Not him.

God, now what?

When she opened her eyes again, Sky was two feet from her face. He seemed to recognize her somehow now. His eyes twitched as he took over Lennox's mind.

Down. Farther in to the darkness she fought against every day—the darkness she let the light shine through. She was weakened by him—his face, his eyes.

188

Childhood memories twisted with lies. If it was any other Prowler, she could break his hold, but this was Sky. *Her* Sky.

Thoughts of evil and hate filled her and she desperately sought after God. God was the only one that could get her through this. He had before. She could not give in to the darkness—neither hers nor Sky's.

She fought against the crippling medicine. Words formed in her heart before they spilled from her mouth. She fumbled over them.

"Sky, you… *have*… to fight… this." She took a breath. Her words were feeble. "This is not you. It's the drugs in your system. It's Ahab. Sky, I know you're in there." She gathered enough strength to speak louder. "Please. *Fight!*" Sky's eyes twitched again, switching from Prowler eyes to Sky's green eyes. "That's it. You can do this. Fight the evil with good. God is on your side."

Ahab's fists curled into balls. Sky's ability to override the venom in his system changed the game. His eyes were a tell-tale sign that he fought against the Prowler venom. It was a tell-tale sign of faith.

"What a disappointment." Ahab grit his teeth. "Sal, take him back to the lab." He motioned for the scientist to come and remove Sky from the room. "We will need to break him more," Ahab added before he took the thin needle off of the vinyl record, instantly stopping the Anthem from playing in the room.

Lennox sighed, relieved for a moment. She understood all too well that next time it would be harder to free Sky from his trance. Ahab would "break him more." Sky was already too broken and her heart broke right along with him.

Infuriating anger rippled through Lennox's muscles, giving her enough strength to barely move the laboratory table she was strapped to. Ahab noticed and wrapped a hand around her throat—not tight enough to choke her, but not loose enough for her to breathe normally.

"You will tell me what the locket does and help me use it against the Sparrow tech. My scientists can't break the code to the locket, but they *can* and *will* break Sky more. I will break him until there is nothing left. Is that what you want?"

Lennox knew deep in her heart that no matter what

she did, Ahab would experiment on Sky regardless, so she shook her head, "No" and bit her tongue until she drew blood.

"Fine, have it your way. I… "Ahab held a pasty hand to his chest while keeping the other around her neck. "I did not want to do this. But, it looks like I have to."

Ahab released Lennox's vocal chords and walked toward an intercom on the wall. He pressed the button and yelled, "Sal!"

The scientist took only a minute to return. "Yes sir?"

"Prepare the strongest, most potent venom." Ahab looked back at Lennox to make sure she overheard every single deliberate word.

"*Sir*, we are only in phase one of testing Venom VI. It will most likely cause severe mutations, causing our work to go awry." Sal pursed his lips. "It is not the result you wished to seek."

Ahab's eyes filled with rage. "Are you questioning my command?" He squared his shoulders, standing tall over the scientist.

Sal shrunk back. "No… no, sir. Uh… not at all. I

only wanted to make you aware..." The Regime scientist glanced at the motionless Lennox strapped upright to the table. "Is it for Miss Winters?"

Ahab let out a hard laugh, causing him to cough. "No, no, no, no. I need her fully functional. Let's top off Sky's dose." Ahab's eyes peered over his shoulder to see Lennox's response.

"It will kill him," Sal said matter-of-factly.

It had to be a ploy. Would Ahab *really* kill one of his precious genetically enhanced specimens? Lennox did not want to risk it.

"Give it to me, not Sky. Please." Better her than her best friend. He had been through enough.

"No, that won't do. It's for Sky. Sal, get to it." Ahab's brows scrunched together.

"No!" Lennox pushed the word out with a heavy breath.

Ahab threw a question at Lennox like a dagger. "Are you ready to tell me how to activate the locket against the Sparrows now?"

"Never," Lennox whispered.

"Fine. You've wasted enough of my time. Sal, make sure Sky receives the Venom within the hour."

Ahab snapped his fingers. "Chop, chop!"

Sal ran out of the room like a scared dog.

Lennox cried out from within. *Lord, You have to intervene. I can't do this without You.*

Chapter 21

There was no way Lennox would help Ahab. Not today. Not ever.

Ahab foolishly allowed the sedative to run completely out of her system. He said she needed to be at "full mental capacity," and she was. More than he knew. She hatched a plan of escape and hoped for a chance to use it.

She sorted her options. Unlike when she was in the impossible pit, the white-walled room offered opportunity for escape. If she planned it right, she could bolt out the door and hope for the best, except then she would have to find the locket on her own. She already had to find Sky. No, she would let the guards lead her straight to its location. Eventually, the guards would unstrap her from the table and have to apply some sort of shackle. Then they would lead her straight to the locket where she planned to fight, break free, and grab it. Once she escaped, she would free Sky from his lab table and pray for God to take over. Only God could cleanse the heart and mind. Of course, the plan's execution would not be that simple, but it did allow the chance for the Regime to make an error. They were evil, not invincible. With God on her side, anything was possible.

It took hours for the potent medicine to seep through her muscles and out of her system. As her body fully came back to life, she stretched against the straps and moved her head from side to side to loosen the knots in her neck. The prolonged periods without moving caused soreness in every inch of her, but it did not dull her wit. Her mind never quit. She continually stretched out her restrained limbs as she patiently waited for her captors.

Just as she suspected, four guards came to transport her to the locket. Lennox studied their movements and, to her surprise, realized one of them was a woman. Lennox had not seen many female Regime soldiers. At least *she* would be a fair match for

Lennox—unlike the men whose shoulders were broad with muscles. They were sure to be a tough match for anyone, let alone a one-hundred-and-thirty-pound girl. Lennox hoped she could run faster than them because that would be her greatest chance of escape.

Unless... unless, maybe I could reach for one of their weapons before the others could draw their own.

That was wishful thinking, of course. Lennox was a good shot, but probably not that good... yet. A few more years of training and she could be. It would be better if she was more seasoned in battle, but her current skill-set mixed with sheer hope would have to do.

The female guard unstrapped all of Lennox's restraints. She looked down at the unfamiliar soldier. Her face was hidden by a black cap, which was why Lennox thought she was a man at first. She read the tag on the soldier's uniform—Calland.

Lennox wondered who Calland was before she became a Regime soldier. Did she have dreams of becoming something else? The female soldier looked to be in her late twenties, as did the male soldiers. How long had they been the Regime? Had they always been

196

on Ahab's side?

Questions rambled in Lennox's mind until the last strap was undone, then every ounce of her ignited and became fully aware of her surroundings.

The three male soldiers aimed their weapons at Lennox while Calland applied strange electronic shackles to her wrists and ankles.

So much for running faster.

The shackles sparked to life when Calland pushed the button in her left hand. The new restraints radiated heat and glowed bright red against Lennox's skin.

This is going to be harder than I thought.

Calland led her with one man on each side and the third behind them. Ahab covered all his bases. He put himself in Lennox's shoes, forcing himself to think as she thought. He could not take her plan of escape away, but he could make it harder.

The halls were long and tight. The two guards on each side could barely walk without bumping in to the walls. Lennox wanted so badly to shove them and lunge for Calland. She would place her shackled wrists around her neck, turning her into a human shield as she twisted her body around away from the guard behind.

Not yet.

It wasn't time. Lennox patiently waited for an opportunity closer to the locket's location.

The guard behind her placed the barrel of his gun into her back and shoved.

"Almost there, keep moving." His baritone voice could be as soothing as a lullaby if it wasn't for the gun to her back.

She took two hurried steps to remove the barrel from her spine.

Calland placed her hand on a screen in the wall. A crimson digital image of her prints appeared before the wall slid into itself. Lennox would have walked right past it without a second glance. Good thing she waited to bolt.

Behind the wall, one of several hanging metal bridges connected the floor they stood on to a laboratory in the center—the only way to access it. Below them was pitch black darkness. Lennox assumed the lab was suspended from the top floor of the high rise—the hardest floor to get to.

The hardest floor to escape.

Perfect.

The metal bridge was too narrow for the guards to walk beside Lennox, so two went before her, and two after. Every step she took with her bare feet felt too heavy against the grated metal. The sound of shifting bolts and swaying steel made Lennox want off the bridge as fast as possible. She walked close to the guard in front of her until her feet hit the cold floor of the lab.

When she looked up, she saw the locket.

And Sky.

Hope rushed through her veins.

Chapter 22

Sky lay on a metal operating table connected to tubes of yellow venom. A white blanket covered him from the waist down and his head and wrists were strapped tight. The rest of him glistened with sweat as his muscles twitched involuntarily. His eyes were closed.

Lennox hated seeing him in this state. He looked so helpless—unlike when he was awake. He terrified her when he was alert and Prowler-like.

Answerless questions ran rampant inside her. Could he return from being taken so far? Was the deepest darkness in him too much to come back from? How would Sky fare after so many doses?

She noticed the man's figure near Sky.

Ahab stood at his bedside, reading a tech screen. Lennox rushed toward him and pushed past Calland, who pressed a button on a remote. Electricity shot through her entire body, making a thousand tiny pricks run across every inch of her skin. Lennox stutter-stepped backward in pain and almost fell. She stumbled in shock as she regained her footing, and then peered back at Calland with grit teeth.

Calland waved the remote trigger in the air. "I wouldn't."

She rolled her eyes and shifted her focus back to Ahab. Lennox had reacted impulsively.

"You're going to kill him!" Lennox shouted. "It's too much!"

Ahab hardly moved. She was aware Ahab didn't care about what she said, but she had to try something. Anything. She would do whatever she had to in order to save Sky. Ahab just didn't want to lose his precious Prowler. He seemed to care about his monsters in a weird, narcissistic way.

Ahab turned around smugly.

"On the contrary, *you* are killing him." He held the screen to his chest. He bit his bottom lip and smacked his tongue. "Help me, and I will stop the Venom VI that is being pumped in to him. It's your choice, of course." He grinned like the grim reaper.

"How do I know you'll keep your word?" Lennox's face scrunched. "How do I know you won't just kill me after I activate it?" She was sure it wasn't that simple. The Regime wouldn't just let the two of them walk out together and go merrily on their way. There was *always* an agenda.

"You can't know for sure. Either do or don't. I am tiring of you altogether." Ahab turned back around and looked at his tech screen, then typed in a code that made the monitors scream with loud beeps. The alarm silenced after a few seconds.

Lennox suspected he did this to get a rise out of her.

Her eyes scanned the suspended laboratory. There was not much room for escape. She could only run to one of the five narrow, metal bridges. Each of them extended to a different side of the pentagon shaped walls— walls that towered above what she thought was the building's summit.

"This way." Calland led Lennox to the locket's location.

The locket was encased in an acrylic box that sat on a lighted table. Lennox wanted to reach out, take it, release Sky, and run, but the shackles prevented her. The guards would shoot her down anyway. Her options dwindled further. She had to choose between helping Ahab or activating the locket. *No.* She must escape before Sky slipped into Prowler oblivion.

Ahab strolled to the table, resting his hands against it. His hands looked as if he stuck them in a pot of boiling water and sustained second-degree burns. Lennox studied his face. It was red and raw. Painful looking blisters polka-dotted his neck. She had not noticed their severity under previous lighting. His skin had to feel like it was on fire, though he might enjoy the pain. Lennox wouldn't put it past him.

Ahab spoke. "My scientists suspect that the locket will destroy the dome that covers Sparrow City and the other cities like it."

Lennox's countenance fell. He knew about the other cities—the safe havens for Defiers. She hoped he didn't know about the one Annabeth and James were in.

"That's right, Lennox." The evil Regime Commander continued with a grin. "I know about those little cities as well. Now!" He slammed his fist on the table. "Help me... and I'll help Sky."

Lennox pondered his request. She could never

allow Ahab free entry into Sparrow City—or any other that held innocent people. He would kill everyone and destroy everything just like he had everywhere else. She wasn't going to let any more civilians fall prey to his corrupt vendetta.

She nodded her head, glanced at Sky, and then back at the locket. She pretended to examine it, biding time. She opened the acrylic box, reaching in to grasp the locket in her shackled hands. The pictures of her and Oliver had been removed. The chain had been mended from when Ahab ripped it from her neck, but her mother's favorite scripture, "We walk by faith, not by sight" had been scratched off the gold. Rough, smudged, yellow metal was now in its place.

Lennox furrowed her brows. "What did your scientists do to it?" It didn't matter. The power wasn't in the gold. It was in the words and her belief in the words. She couldn't see a way out of this predicament, but she believed there would be a way somehow.

Ahab squeezed Lennox's shoulder and tightened his jaw. "Hurry up and do something with it already."

Lennox swallowed. "I'm trying."

Time. She needed more time. Time to think… to

204

think of something more she could do to draw out the minutes and hold Ahab off.

Ahab pulled the locket out of her hands to look at it, inspecting every part. He put the locket back in Lennox's palm. "Quit stalling."

Lennox rubbed the gold between her hands. A piece of metal where a picture usually lay shifted. Her father made sure that only her fingerprints could do that. Lennox felt the microchip underneath her thumb.

"I need tools." She remained calm, sliding the moveable gold back in to position over the chip. She needed to figure it all out. *What's my next move?* She bit her bottom lip and waited.

Ahab exhaled. "Sal will get you what you need. You have an hour." He turned to walk away but spun on his heel to say one more thing. "Guards, stay alert. Calland, burn her to a crisp if she tries to escape. I will just have her brother give it a go next."

Lennox's heart fell. "You have Oliver?"

She stood straight up and peered in to Ahab's beady eyes. He smiled, calmly turned, and then walked out of sight.

Sal brought a kit and placed it on the table where

Lennox worked. She scattered the tools across the table. One of which, Lennox was sure an adaptor blade. The Regime must have started to steal Sparrow technology. And Sal wouldn't have known not to give Lennox one while working on the locket, shackled, with four armed guards. She muttered scripture under her breath as she pretended to work diligently on the locket.

"No weapon formed against us shall prosper."

Her vision blurred.

Something wasn't right.

Lennox was awake but she could not see. She braced herself by holding the table. It felt like an earthquake took place, but she didn't know what the bright light and deafening noise that came with it was. She heard muffled sounds around her and felt the locket in her right hand. She held it tight as she felt around the table in front of her. She no longer felt shackles on her wrists or ankles.

What?

Her eyes slowly focused and allowed light in.

Calland lay on the ground—unconscious—with the control to the shackles still in her hand. When she fell, she must have hit the button to deactivate them because they were at Lennox's feet, a non-threatening white. The other three guards did not fare as well. They were covered in their own blood, smashed by a heavy metal beam. They couldn't get up if they tried.

The laboratory rumbled again. The metal swayed against itself, screeching.

Lennox carefully clasped the locket around her neck and raced to Sky's surgical table. His skin was more yellow than before. The venom dripped from the IVs into his system, changing him from the inside out.

Too much.

"Sky!" Lennox tried to wake him. She brushed his sweaty hair to the side as she leaned over him. Nothing. He wouldn't move or open his eyes. Tears formed, but she refused to let them fall. She threw the blanket on the floor. White, silver trimmed pants covered him to his ankles. At least the scientists had the decency to clothe him. She scrambled to get the tubes out of his body.

Nine.

Nine tubes pumped poison in to his bloodstream. She shook her head. He was too heavy to carry.

The wires that suspended the bridges began to pop, making haunted whistling noises as they did. Everything wobbled. Flames whipped against the lab's equipment. Vials of Ahab's precious venom exploded with quick bursts of hazy orange. Smoke floated in the air.

Lennox saw gray Sparrow uniforms in the distance. She rubbed her eyes in disbelief. Her own receptors deceived her. Maybe her neuro system was damaged from the toxins.

She kept hope alive as she refocused on Sky, dragging him off the table. His body thumped against metal. Lennox struggled to pull his body five feet.

The two remaining bridges seemed an eternity away. With a long step back, followed by a pull, she gave one tug at a time toward that eternity.

Again… and again… and again.

Moans came from Sky's otherwise lifeless body.

The sound of crackling fire and weapons blasting obliterated the screeching metal. Lennox moved faster, reaching the wall. The wall's digital screen was the only obstacle keeping Lennox and Sky in the laboratory. Her hand could not open it.

Calland's would.

Lennox crawled over Sky and raced down the bridge. Smoke made her vision murky. She found the lighted table near Calland's unconscious body.

She was gone.

Oh God! Where did she go? Give me strength.

The three other soldiers remained on the ground.

Lennox scanned the room, unable to see past the black and green fog. The chemicals in the lab made everything worse. Her head grew heavy from the gas produced by burning liquids. She blinked hard to clear her vision, but it left her eyes in terrible pain. She had to get out, fast. The gas was too dangerous to breathe and too hard to see through.

Lennox heard movement to her left.

Black fatigues.

The blur cleared.

The lean, female Regime soldier stood ten feet away with a handgun pointed at Lennox's chest. Lennox felt exposed and vulnerable in just her cotton shirt and leggings. She was defenseless against the agitated soldier. Calland kept the gun aimed at Lennox as she walked closer. Lennox backed away, one tiny step at a time. Her feet slid across the metal grated floor that vibrated.

"You should have killed us when you had the chance," Calland said, now five feet away.

Lennox felt her heart pound. She stood directly in the crosshairs of a thin, red laser that marked the gun's intention. Calland couldn't miss.

"I'm not like you. I don't kill people just because I can." Lennox backed up to the lighted table, trying to keep Calland distracted. The tools still lie on her former workspace, and she hoped to grab the adaptor blade.

The angry girl with fire in her eyes and a gun in her hand crept forward. "You're foolish and you've chosen the wrong side."

"Have I?"

Lennox's hand fumbled over several other tools before she found the resourceful blade. The tech transformed to a long metal baton—the kind that crushed the back of Lennox's knees when she refused to bow. She swung it around quickly and with force.

The gun fired one shot before it clanked against the steel floor. The bullet lodged into a screen behind her.

Lennox's heartrate jumped.

Too close.

Calland huffed, then charged at Lennox with a scream. Lennox thrusted the baton against Calland's knees which sent her down hard in a fit of rage. The Regime soldier moaned as she grabbed hold of the metal Sparrow-designed tech. Lennox wrestled to regain control. Both women fell to the ground.

Calland sat on Lennox's torso with the baton shoved against her throat. The grated grooves of the cold metal floor scratched against Lennox's shoulder blades as she twisted and turned to get leverage. She finally gathered enough strength to hurl Calland from on top of her, but lost control of the adaptor blade in the process.

Calland twirled the baton in her hand. "Told you, wrong side." She glowered with a snarl.

Lennox shifted her gaze. Calland followed Lennox's eyes to the gun and peered back at her.

"I wouldn't," she said.

Lennox scrambled for the gun. Calland's footfalls

were heavy for her size. Although noise was everywhere, Lennox could hear a pin drop. The adrenaline pulsed beneath her skin as she raised the weapon and met Calland's gaze two feet from her.

Stay strong, Lennox. Don't hesitate. Do what you have to do.

"You already said you wouldn't kill me." Calland smirked, stepping closer, unfazed. The red dot was positioned directly on her forehead. She crept closer, shaking the molecular structure of the adaptor blade into a knife. Lennox had never hated the amazing technology, until now.

Lennox hid her nerves and hoped her voice wouldn't shake. *"Wrong.* I said I wouldn't if I didn't have to." She had been told that she had a good poker face. It worked.

Calland stopped where she was, expressing the will to live. Lennox knew Calland would kill her if given the chance. She wouldn't give it to her.

Gripping the gun tighter, Lennox continued, "Now, move slowly down that bridge." She tilted her head to the suspended bridge that Sky was on. She narrowed her eyes. "Move, now!" The authority in her voice even surprised herself.

Calland started to walk. "You know, there's too much venom in him. He won't survive. And even if he does... he's gone." Calland looked over her shoulder and twisted her lip into a sickening smile that looked a lot like Ahab's.

"Don't talk." Lennox shoved Calland with her left hand, keeping the gun pointed at her with her right.

Calland took two fumbling steps forward, and then kept a steady pace. By the time they reached Sky, he was convulsing. Foam came from his mouth. Lennox's heart sank.

"See." Calland looked down at Sky. "Gone." The woman showed no sympathy or remorse. She was an unsympathetic monster.

Lennox swallowed her fear and refused to believe Calland's words. God was able to deliver Sky. It wasn't about how things looked.

We walk by faith, not by sight. God, I need You.

Lennox refocused and curled her free hand into a fist to help her stay on track. She waved the gun between the screen and Calland. "The door."

Calland placed her hand on the screen and a beam

of red light ran up and down. Lennox held the gun tighter. Her mind raced with anxious thoughts. The door slid open to eerie stillness.

Calland took her opportunity to flee and shoved Lennox hard, almost pushing her over the railing. Lennox caught her balance right before she tumbled off the bridge. With a pounding heart, she secured her footing and let out an exhausted huff, then held on to the rail for a moment to calm herself. Nothing but darkness waited to greet her down there. She stepped in to the narrow hall, hoping to stop Calland. She needed Calland's hand to open doors, but the Regime soldier was already halfway down another corridor. The chase wasn't worth it. Lennox would do it without her. She had to. Her and Sky's life depended on it.

Things seemed too quiet in the Regime's hall.

What is going on? Where is everyone?

There were no guards, no scientists, and Ahab was nowhere in sight. How did he manage to escape? Would his time ever come?

Lennox looked back at the dangling laboratory that was now quiet and empty. There wasn't time to figure out what was happening. She had to get Sky somewhere safe.

Lennox exhaled, tucked the gun in the waistband of her leggings, and pulled Sky over the threshold.

Chapter 23

Sky and Lennox were open targets in the hall. They'd be goners once someone finally noticed them. Calland seemed like the type to hold a grudge and she would come back with reinforcements. Lennox did not know how long they had until their luck ran out.

She could not move Sky much farther. She twisted her body in search of the next open door—somewhere they could hide out until she thought of a better plan— a realistic one. She propped him up against the wall, checking the doors closest to them.

Lennox hit the digital hand reading screen with the butt of the gun, exposing the hidden wires behind it. She fumbled with the blue one first to see if any walls slid open or any doors unlocked. It did nothing. She moved to the yellow wire, attaching it to a sensor. A lab room door opened.

Men and women on laboratory tables were lined up in rows, dressed in white and silver like little lab rats. IVs dripped a concoction of milky liquid into them, keeping them asleep. Lennox cringed. It was haunting. They were probably next in line to become the most advanced Prowlers. Even Dr. Frankenstein would have a problem with this. As much as she hated it, the disturbing room was their only option. Lennox hoped the room of sleeping monsters would not be their end.

She wrapped her arms under Sky's armpits and pulled him through the door as her muscles screamed in pain. She searched the room for extra weapons, but the lab's contents were useless. Needles and beakers wouldn't help in a gunfight.

She slid her back down the wall next to where Sky leaned, unconscious. Every once in a while someone twitched, causing Lennox to jump. She couldn't stay in the room forever.

She held the gun out in front of her and removed the clip. Three bullets. She slid the clip back in place. She wouldn't kill anyone—that's not what she thought God wanted. However, she would continue to defend herself. If she had to shoot someone to survive, she would. She took a deep breath, looked up, and asked

God for help. "God, I don't know what to do. Please, give me wisdom." A calm presence resided over Lennox. She inhaled deeply and closed her eyes to listen to the still, small voice within her heart. *Movement is life.* She had to move for Sky's sake and her own.

She leaned her forehead against Sky's temple. "I will come back for you," she whispered, kissing him gently on the cheek as she choked back tears. She stood and walked toward the exit. With her hand on the door, she looked one last time at a sleeping Sky and forced herself in to the hall.

The chaos on the other side of the door startled her. Frantic scientists in white lab coats ran the halls with vials of venom in their hands and Regime soldiers chased after them as if they ran from something. They would never want to lose all their years of work. Lennox hadn't heard any of the commotion. The lab must have been soundproof. Lennox tried to get lost in the crowd as men and women carelessly shoved her in to the center of the stampede without notice. She glanced over her shoulder and saw the pursuing threat.

Sparrows.

Not the uniformed soldier kind, but the realistic, flying robotic kind. These sparrows must be weapons sent by Sparrow City scientists.

Thousands of unnaturally large bird-shaped drones sprayed the halls with the blue bullets. Regime soldiers in black fatigues fell to the ground as the liquid caused them to twist and turn in agonized defeat. The robotic birds immobilized the enemy, just as the Sparrow scientists intended. Lennox couldn't afford to be trampled—or worse—shot by her own side, so she ran with the crowd until she fell to the side of a narrow, open hallway. She caught her breath and watched the Sparrow drones follow the Regime.

They're here! They have to be here.

Lennox ran down the hallway in search of help and hope. The stealth jets must have made it, and Sparrows would be there.

Somewhere.

Lennox slowed her pace at the sight of an oncoming body.

Friend or foe? She was about to find out.

The tall silhouette of a man inched closer to where she walked. As he got closer, Lennox saw the uniform he wore.

Foe.

She drew her weapon and held it up to the man, aiming it at his leg. Her finger rested on the trigger.

He wasn't a man. He was just a boy, really, and younger than her at fourteen... maybe fifteen-years-old. She didn't want to shoot him at all, but she had no tech to protect her and nothing else to go off of. If he made a move, she had to.

The teenage boy drew his weapon in reply and his red laser crept to Lennox's chest. She couldn't let it happen.

"Forgive me." She pulled the trigger.

The bullet hit his thigh. He dropped his weapon as his hands grabbed his wound. He fell to his knees, and then to the floor. His eyes remained on the gun.

"Don't." Lennox shook her head and kicked the gun away from him. "I need your boots."

The boy struggled to unlace his boots with his bloody fingers. He managed to get them off and threw them in front of her. She slipped them on one at a time, keeping the gun aimed at him. He watched her.

She swallowed the guilt from causing his injury

and darted past without looking back.

"Lord, please let him discover who You are."

She ran faster, her booted feet clunked against the floor. A round of bullets from the boy soldier she had just shot chased her down the hall. He had not forgiven her.

Lennox turned a slight right in to another passageway as shrapnel ricocheted off the walls. There was no time to think. She had to move. She followed a new path down a darkened hall. No lights guided her. It was the darkest place in the stronghold. She wished she had Sparrow night vision tech to help her see.

She heard faint screams and footfalls. She was close to something.

Moving forward, she kept her hand wrapped around the gun that only had two bullets left. Two more foes and she'd be out of ammunition.

Chapter 24

Fluorescent lights flashed on and off. Lennox looked at the two-way mirrors as she ran past room after room of equipment and laboratory beds. How many Prowlers was Ahab going to make?

She was lost and alone. She found her way down an empty stairwell and opened the door to a new hall. Help had to be close. She promised herself she could go down one more hallway before she turned around.

She ran down the new corridor to a dead end. She paused.

Her spirit urged her forward, so she obeyed. She touched the handle to a black steel door while looking at the flashing screen to the right of it. She smashed the glass and fidgeted with the wires as she did the one before, hoping she would have the same luck. She knew it wasn't really luck at all. God made a way, and she prayed He would again.

"God will lead, if only you'd follow," General Eli

would say. So she decided to follow the still, small voice in her heart guiding her and continued to fiddle with the wires.

Crash!

Shots fired. Her hands shook.

No combination seemed to work. Not the blue to the yellow or the yellow to the red. She let out a heavy breath. She couldn't give up! She had come too far to turn back. She trusted God, no matter what. Somehow, He would see her through.

Voices coming from down the hall made Lennox move faster. "Come on," she said as her hands fumbled over wires. The voices got closer. Lennox had nowhere to run and nowhere to hide. She turned to see whom the voices belonged to. She braced herself with her left shoulder against the wall and gripped the gun with both of her hands.

The lights flashed on, then off, as blue lasers shined against the walls. She couldn't believe her eyes. She looked closer and threw her head back in relief. A Sparrow team marched toward her. She ran toward them in the hall with the gun at her side.

"Thank God," she said as she hurried closer to

them.

The team trained their weapons on her with their blue lasers aimed at her chest. She halted.

Lennox dropped her gun and lifted her hands in the air. "Whoa! Whoa! Whoa! I'm a Sparrow. My name is Lennox Winters."

The team of seven in gray jumpsuits approached. "Lennox Winters?" They pulled her between them for safety.

"Yes," she said, looking behind their helmets. Fearless eyes met her stare.

"I'm Faulkner, we're Team Three," one said, signaling the team to advance ahead. "Sorry, no time for formalities, we gotta keep moving. Your brother sent us in for you."

"Oliver? Where is he?" Lennox stayed by Faulkner's side behind the team.

"He's with the medics."

The eight of them took deliberate steps as they cautiously crept forward.

Medics?

"Is he okay? What happened?" Lennox anxiously asked.

"We rescued him and Easton on the ground floor. A firefight broke out. He took a bullet to the knee and almost fought me to come with us to get you. He'll be fine."

"And Easton?"

"Fine. That woman has nine lives." Faulkner continued forward.

Lennox slowed and reached out to Faulkner. "My partner, Sky, he's on an upper level in a laboratory."

"I'll send three of my men to get him. What level?"

Lennox hesitated. If she told him the truth, he may not be as willing to help, but she couldn't lie. Faulkner deserved the truth, no matter how hard it was to process.

"The very top. But there's something I should tell you..."

"What is it?" Faulkner held his weapon up and pointed it from one side to another, lighting the dust filled halls with a narrow beam of blue light. "There's no time to waste."

The other Sparrows did the same. Beams of blue stabbed through the dust, giving an ambient glow to the halls when the light flicked off as they steadily crept forward in the darkness.

Lennox mustered the courage to say the words she didn't even want to say out loud as she carefully watched his reaction. "They turned him in to a Prowler."

He stopped, holding his fist in the air. "Winters, we can't go after a Prowler. They're too dangerous."

"He's one of us. He's not one of them, not really." Lennox held her breath. She did not blame Faulkner, but she could not leave Sky—even if he was in Prowler form. "If you don't go back for him, I will."

Faulkner shook his head. "You don't have any gear." He spoke in to his com. "Ross, Mercer, and Grant." Three men gathered close to Faulkner, waiting for an order. "Top level. Find Sky Conners and bring him home. Be on guard, the Prowler venom is in his blood."

"Yes sir!" The three men turned to leave. They didn't even blink twice. They did not care that Sky had Prowler venom in his blood. They would bring him home.

"Thank you," Lennox said.

Faulkner nodded. "Our next mission is to get you to the locket, then to the main frame."

"I have the locket." Lennox took it off from around her neck and held it up.

"Then let's get you to the main frame," Faulkner concluded.

As he led, the three remaining Sparrows surrounded Lennox. They went down too many flights of stairs to count. With each flight down, another perilous war confronted them. The Sparrows raised their Sapphire Shields and fired off round after round, leaving dozens of men immobilized in their wake. Adrenaline melded with purpose and gave Lennox the motivation to continue. Her feet rubbed raw with every step in her oversized boots.

Faulkner stayed in the lead. "When we reach the basement, be prepared for a bigger fight. Two more flights and we'll be there."

They crept past Regime soldiers who were bound by the blue Sparrow serum. The ones who still managed to speak begged to be released from its grasp. Eventually they would be once the other Sparrows locked them away for their crimes against humanity and God. They would even be given an opportunity to turn from their wicked ways—though, not many chose that route.

One Regime soldier tried to reach out to Lennox but his hand twisted back into himself. His judgment had come. The consequence of living in evil was far worse than death. Lennox still could not understand what drove people to the Regime. She shook the image of the Regime soldier away and moved forward.

The team continued down to the very depths of the building. Lennox calmed her breathing and clutched the locket in her fist. Everything came down to this. She watched as Team Three ran their hands against the walls.

"There's a door along this wall." Faulkner ran his fingers over the seamless part of the steel wall.

"Jackson." Faulkner motioned for the slender man with a narrow nose and closely set eyes to come forward. "Do you think you can breach it?"

"Yes sir." Jackson brought out a tech screen and typed a code onto the device.

Two Regime soldiers appeared and wasted no time firing at the invading Sparrows. Team Three shot back.

"Any day now, Jackson!" Faulkner shouted over the firefight. "Here." Faulkner handed Lennox a Sapphire Shield.

Lennox activated it and the smooth, clear shield formed. Two more soldiers encroached on the tightening space. Lennox guarded Jackson and made herself small behind the shield to avoid being shot. Bullets bounced off the sapphire. Faulkner stood in front and fired back, keeping everyone covered. A piece of steel slid open.

"Done." Jackson tucked his tech screen under his arm.

Two Sparrows entered first, shooting the Regime soldiers inside with their Strikers. Their bodies coiled within themselves as they all fell to the ground.

"Clear!"

"Alright, Lennox. You're up." Faulkner guarded her as she walked through the opening to the main frame. "Jackson, shut us in."

Faulkner stood between the threshold of the door and hall. The number of Regime soldiers multiplied.

"Jackson!" Faulkner yelled and took a step back.

"I'm on it, sir." Jackson tapped his tech screen

fervently and the door slid shut.

Finally.

Lennox stood before the Regime's main frame. Hard drives, holograms, and large screens covered every inch of the room. She opened the locket and moved the gold plate that sat on top of the microchip with her thumb.

This was it.

Just get it close enough, the nanobytes will do the rest.

She inserted the chip in to one of the hard drives.

Nothing.

She gulped and for a moment panicked. Her head throbbed as she searched her brain for what she had missed or done wrong.

Then… everything.

The nanobytes turned in to a thousand tiny tech spiders that ran along the entire system—inside, outside, everywhere. The mainframe went ballistic. Screens blacked out and hard drives let out smoke.

Her dad had done it. She had done it.

It worked.

Chapter 25

The ceiling above cracked. The walls quaked and the ground beneath shook.

"They're going to blow the place," Faulkner said.

"How are we going to get out?" Lennox asked.

"The way we got in." Faulkner moved to the door and readied his gun. The others joined him.

"Sir, my screen is reading over a dozen heat signatures out there." Jackson stared at his screen.

"Do it, Jackson," Faulkner ordered.

Jackson's face grew concerned as he typed, making the door open. It slid slowly and revealed guns and glowing eyes. Faulkner fired several shots and hit three before a Prowler took hold of his mind. He fell to the ground, holding his head as if in excruciating pain.

This can't be happening! We've come too far.

Lennox stepped back behind the smoking hard drives. She had no offensive weapon to fire back at the Regime—only the Sapphire Shield stood between her and the flying bullets. She held the shield in front of her as blasts erupted and bullets rained. There was only one way to survive a Prowler attack.

Pray.

Sparrows fired their weapons and the Regime theirs. Lennox bowed to God in the midst of chaos, completely surrendered to God's will. The situation seemed hopeless. Impossible. If she died now, she would willingly die. She had fulfilled her purpose. Her destiny was complete. But God worked best with the impossible. He could get her out.

"I trust You."

As she prayed, the whole world stopped spinning. Only she and God existed. There was no war, no Prowlers, only peace.

She opened her eyes.

Sky stood before her, eyes glowing. She swallowed hard.

Did she trust God enough?

The building fell around them and time stood still. He towered over her for what felt like forever.

One second… two seconds… a minute.

He did not move. She rose and lowered the shield,

looking directly in to Sky's eyes.

Lennox's peripheral vision translated the chaos around them, though it did not feel real. Flames whipped against the walls and the sound of bullets pierced through the air. The oxygen turned black.

Her brain snapped her back to reality. Lennox choked to breathe. She returned her focus to her best friend, waiting for him to attack.

In a split second, Sky picked her up from the ground and ran. His eyes flickered between Prowler and Sky... *her* Sky. She saw the fight in his soul. He shook his head violently in an attempt to stay himself and ran faster than humanly possible out of the Regime's main frame. Lennox dangled in his arms. He shoved anyone and everything out of his way with his shoulder, protecting Lennox at all costs. He ran up and over the stairs and debris, then up again.

Lennox fell out of Sky's arms and onto the earth. Fire rained down as the building exploded in smoke with one loud blast. She turned on the ground to look back at Sky who lay helpless a few feet away. Twisted metal and shards of glass covered his legs.

He got her out before the collapse of the mirrored

high-rise. He was able to save her, but not himself.

Lennox shot up and ran to him. She watched the pain in his eyes vanish and fill with peace. Sky shook his head and pointed up.

She looked at the night sky and watched in awe as the stars fell from the heavens and the world around them went up in flames. The Word of God appeared as if He wrote the words with His own fingers on a parchment of atmosphere.

In the last days, I will pour out my Spirit on all flesh.

When one truth finished, another took its place.

For God so loved the world that He gave His one and only begotten Son...

Peace rushed over Lennox. "There's no stopping the move of God, is there?" she whispered as she held on to Sky's hand.

No matter how many Bibles the Regime burned, no matter how hard they tried to get rid of the truth, God's Word lived. Jesus lived. He was tried and true. No one and nothing could stop Him. God was truly at work in the midst of this terrible war.

A cloud of dust floated up as the building

continued to shift, falling more with every second. Drones buzzed in the air, causing Lennox to look away from the miracle. She refocused on how she would get Sky out of danger. Tears fell from his eyes.

"I'm going to get you out," she assured him.

He convulsed, shook his head, and then stopped completely. He looked directly at her.

"Run!" he whispered. His eyes dimmed.

No!

Lennox wiped his tears away. "I'm not leaving you. I won't do it."

Sky's eyes grew wild and his face contorted as he succumbed to the venom in his veins.

The Prowler returned.

Lennox wrenched her hand away to avoid Sky's crushing, strong hands. She backed out of his reach.

"Fight it, Sky. You have to fight it!"

Lennox went into shock. She held her hand up to her shoulder and rocked in pain. She smelled it before she saw it. She held her hand out in front of her.

Blood.

Her shoulder burned. The warm, red liquid dripped down her side and her arm. She sat in a trance, trying to comprehend what just happened. She felt strong hands pull her away. Her feet kicked against the ground as she fought to return to Sky.

"Lennox, we have to go." It was a familiar voice.

Lennox turned to see Ace's face behind a Sparrow helmet. She tried to pull away, ignoring her own pain.

"Look, it's Sky. We can't leave him!" Lennox looked at her fallen best friend.

He wasn't Sky, now. He was all Prowler, fighting to lift the metal off his body.

"He's still in there, Ace, you have to believe me."

Ace moved closer cautiously. "Lennox, Sky took out the three Sparrows sent to rescue him. That's *not* Sky. As much as I hate to say this... he's gone." Lennox ignored him but Ace held her tighter. "He's gone, Lennox!"

"No he's not!" Lennox fought. Ace put his body between her and Sky, blocking her view. "We have to get you help. You're injured."

"He's not gone." Lennox shook her head.

"There's no time."

Ace picked her feet off the ground and pressed a Kev disk onto her undershirt. The tech formed around her body, protecting her from the debris that fell all above them. Lennox beat her right fist against Ace's chest, pounding at his Kev tech.

"We can't just leave him to die!" Tears fell from her eyes as she tried desperately to get free. "Ace! Let me go!" Lennox pushed unsuccessfully.

"No, I am not going to let you get killed too." Ace's southern accent didn't soften the blow.

Killed too?

Sky would never hurt anyone. He wouldn't hurt her. He *saved* her.

Lennox couldn't breathe.

Air!

She needed air. She felt as if she was drowning all over again.

Ace carried her away from the one she loved so dearly.

Sparrows ran toward them. They helped Ace control Lennox and moved in the opposite direction of Sky—the wrong direction.

A scorpion war machine arrived with a dozen more just like it. Lennox watched in horror as she was dragged farther away from the beasts. They unfurled their tails in unison, launching a thousand fiery barbs at the collapsing building. The blasts turned the night sky a hazy orange.

Ace sat her feet down and dragged her by the arm. The ground beneath Lennox's feet seemed to grab hold of her boots, not wanting her to leave or it may have been the heaviness of her heart that weighed the rest of her body down —whatever it was, it hurt. Ace and the others pushed her backward while others pulled her from behind.

She reached out.

A lump formed in her throat. "Sky!"

Sky.

Chapter 26

Ace held Lennox up and kept her from falling. She couldn't feel her body. She couldn't feel anything except crippling knots in her stomach as they pulled her away.

"No!" she cried as they forced her to the stealth jet that waited to depart. It hovered above the destruction, but was too far away from her best friend who was now free from the rubble.

The venom gave Sky more power than Lennox could fathom. He charged toward her with yellow eyes that shone like a feral cat in the night.

A silver ramp stretched to the ground to allow the Sparrows entry. Ace gently marched Lennox up.

Sky was a dozen yards away. Lennox couldn't stop looking at his eyes. Strange noises filled the air. The entire compound lit up bright orange and red. She lost sight of Sky in the smoke.

"Sky!" Lennox pushed and squirmed to get to him

to no avail. *Please, no!*

Ace's strong hands guided her to safety in the jet. The ramp closed, blocking her view. Her right hand went to her temple and pulled her hair as her left dangled, dripping blood. All she had left were those images burned into her brain.

Sky.

Flames.

Smoke.

Ace signaled for a medic to come check Lennox's wound. She did not care about the pain. Her heart hurt more than her shoulder. Everyone around her sounded as if they spoke to her from inside a long tunnel. They were there. She was there—but not really. She saw the Sparrow medic move in slow motion as her senses numbed. They sat her down. She was losing too much blood, too fast.

"Lennox, I am Medic Courtney." Her deep brown eyes looked into Lennox's as she shined a bright white light into them.

Lennox squinted. Courtney pulled supplies from a bag, deactivated the tech, and started to cut away fabric from Lennox's shirt near her shoulder. Lennox blinked hard and tried to regain normalcy within her five senses.

Medic Courtney had a kind face and gentle features, and she worked diligently. She held up a strange new medical instrument filled with a clear liquid.

"This is going to help you heal faster."

She placed the device over Lennox's shoulder and released the medicine. An icy burst of liquid ran through Lennox's veins as if her blood crystallized. Lennox leaned her head back and took in a deep breath. She could see and hear normally again. When she looked back down, Courtney had already removed the bullet. She held it with metal forceps. The bullet clinked against a metal pan.

"Do you want to keep it?" The medic looked quickly at Lennox, then turned back to the injury. She applied the gauze to the wound.

Lennox tilted her head. "The bullet?" She turned on the seat she sat on.

"Yeah, some Sparrows like to keep the bullets as tokens of their story. Tokens that remind them how far God has brought them—how they should've been dead but made it out alive. You surely can relate to that."

"Sure, I guess," Lennox replied.

She needed as many reminders as she could get. The bullet would be as a solemn reminder to her friend's sacrifice and God's strength. If only it could bring back Sky like a magic wand.

The medic rinsed the bullet off with saline solution and handed it to Lennox. "Here," she said, holding it out between her thumb and index finger. "Your token."

Lennox wrapped her hand tightly around the little piece of mushroom-shaped metal. "Thank you."

The medic smiled and checked the gauze-wrapped wound one more time then walked away to the others that needed her help.

Lennox tapped her boot against the floor of the jet, staring at the bullet that rested in her palm. It could have killed her, yet here she was *alive*—breathing, fighting... without Sky.

Someone's black boots stood in front of her. She followed the boots all the way up to the man who wore them. Ace hadn't moved. He held on to the cargo straps above him.

"Lennox, I'm sorry." He choked back tears.

"Me too, Ace." Lennox sniffed. "Me too." Her bottom lip quivered. She was sorry she couldn't do more. Sorry she wasn't stronger. Sorry things were the way they were.

Medic Holmes was right. She wanted nothing more than to curl into a ball and cry, but she couldn't. There was more to be done.

"Do you know where my brother is?" Oliver would know what to do.

Ace nodded. "He's on the jet ahead of us. He's worried about you. I let him know you made it on board."

Lennox bit her bottom lip and then tightened her jaw. "Thanks."

Ace took the seat beside her and strapped in as the jet switched from hovering to flight mode. Lennox pulled her harness slowly over her shoulders and buckled in, resting her head back. Tears rolled down her cheeks. Ace glanced her way every so often, smiled slightly, and then lowered his head. Lennox wanted to say something or smile back, but her heart wouldn't let her.

God was able to redeem. He could deliver, restore. She had to trust He would help her flesh believe what her spirit comprehended.

The jet encountered turbulence and Lennox clutched her harness. After a few seconds the jets glided seamlessly through the air again. Her eyelids grew heavy, so she closed them. She must have fallen asleep because when she opened her eyes, the jet was passing through the dome that protected Sparrow City. She looked at Ace. He had conked out too. He pried open his eyes and yawned. Everyone was exhausted.

Lennox let out a heavy sigh as the jet hovered for a moment then gently landed on top of a hill. The ramp opened and the smell of late summer wafted through the air.

Sky loved summer. Before the war he would have been training somewhere on a baseball field.

Lennox sighed and unlatched her harness. Her shoulder was already improved. She could move it slightly without too much pain, though she might need physical therapy to get full range of motion back. Other Sparrows exited first, walking down the ramp to the crowd of Defiers that awaited them. Lennox hesitated

244

to leave the jet. It made everything too real. How could she face the truth?

Ace unlatched himself. He placed a hand on Lennox's back. It startled her and she shivered.

"Sorry." He quickly removed his hand. "Welcome home, Len."

Home.

Would it still feel like home without Sky?

Lennox blamed herself for what happened to him. She thought of things she could have done differently—of how she could have saved him or brought him home. But that didn't matter now. He was gone.

Chapter 27

The next morning, Lennox stood in the very field she wished to return to with Sky. The field seemed empty now, void of the beauty it once held. Gray clouds rolled over Sparrow City.

Fitting.

She had won the battle, but lost Sky, which was as gray as it got.

Eli counted the mission as a victory. They all had. But was it really a victory? It didn't feel like one to Lennox. The storm forming above couldn't compare to the storm within. She tried to hold on to the memory of Sky without his Prowler eyes and lost soul, focusing dearly on the love between them, but it pained her to think of how he was disoriented in his own body. If he survived, he must be fighting it. She saw the fight in his eyes. He could return to himself. He couldn't be gone. It could not happen like this.

Is this really Your plan, Lord? No. I won't believe

that. I can't.

Lennox gulped air. How much more loss could she take?

Lord, my heart hurts. I don't understand Your plan. I hate questioning it, but all I see is death and evil surrounding me, taking what I love.

Lennox cradled her healing shoulder. A Humvee rolled over the hills and straight toward her. She waited with tears that threatened to escape with each breath. Oliver stepped out and made his way to his grieving sister. He had a slight limp in his walk, despite the special high-tech gadget in his knee where the bullet penetrated. He stood before her as a stoic soldier.

"Your knee is healing nicely. I can hardly notice it in your walk." Lennox managed to speak without allowing a downpour of waterworks.

Oliver's eyes widened. "Yeah, new rapid healing technique the scientists taught the medics. It's really a God thing, if you ask me."

She smiled. God spared him and she was grateful. "They used the same stuff on my shoulder. *Definitely* a God thing." Lennox tried to maintain her smile without showing too much heartache.

Oliver pressed his lips together and looked to where the darkened clouds stirred. His eyes met hers. "Len, there's something I want you to see." Oliver slowly reached out his hand, waiting.

Lennox let out a small laugh. "That's exactly what Sky said when he showed me *this* place." She wiped the tear that fell against her curved cheek as she smiled.

The words took her back to Sky in the glowing light of fireflies and the tender moment between them—their friendship and their unbreakable bond.

"There's another place, just as special." Oliver stretched his hand farther out. "Come on." He gave a half smile.

Lennox hesitated, taking one last glance around her favorite place. Her brother led her to the Humvee, opening up the passenger's door for her to enter. She bit the inside of her cheek and sat down on the black seat, peering out the window until Oliver sat on the driver's side.

"Trust me, this place will help you heal." Oliver put the vehicle in gear and they rolled forward.

The dome flickered as hail pounded against it. The same happened inside Lennox. Dark, icy rocks of pain, loss, and hopelessness beat against her every thought and heartbeat. She should compartmentalize like she had been taught, but how could she compartmentalize Sky? She couldn't just shove him to the back of her mind and forget him.

After two miles driven in silence, Oliver stopped the Humvee and turned off the engine.

"We're here," he finally said after a moment of silence.

Lennox looked out the passenger window at something she had never seen in Sparrow City. A small, white wooden chapel sat on top of a hill. How could she have missed it? She never even saw it during physical training.

"The Defiers just built it. We have a few master carpenters who wanted to make it for the returning Sparrows." Oliver answered before she could ask. "We will preserve what we believe... what we know. And I know it's not about the building, but the spot takes you back to a good place, doesn't it?"

"It does." Lennox said, remembering the church she used to attend with her family.

He stepped out of the vehicle and Lennox did the

same. With a heavy sigh, Lennox walked toward the entrance with Oliver. He opened the arched red chapel doors. Wooden pews sat in lines. Ornate stain glass windows were placed every four feet along the walls.

Lennox turned around to Oliver, no longer able to hold it in. "Do you think he made it out?"

Oliver paused, looking like he sincerely gave thought to her question. "I don't know. It looked pretty impossible to survive." He glanced down at the hardwood floor.

"Isn't that where our faith must kick in? *Impossibilities?*" Lennox held on to hope, her heart ached for a miracle. "They say even if he did survive, he's gone. Do you believe that too?" Lennox watched her brother intently, waiting for an ember to ignite. It would be so nice to have someone believe with her.

Oliver nodded and rubbed the bottom of his chin for a second. "I believe God is able." He held his breath a moment longer then spoke again. "All I know is that God can do anything. He can redeem, heal, and restore even the most broken people. And what do we do when the darkness seems closer than the light?"

"We pray," Lennox answered. If she humbled

herself and prayed, God could work in her and the insurmountable odds she faced.

Oliver swallowed hard. "I believe in miracles. I have seen too many not to. Don't lean on man's understanding, not even on mine. Lean on God's." His face released a heaviness that Lennox hadn't noticed before. "Let your desperation build hope within you."

It turned out that Oliver *did* know what to say. He always had.

"I'll give you some time alone. To think. To *pray*." He gave a gentle smile and walked out of the chapel, closing the red doors behind him.

Lennox approached the altar with an anchor of hope bound to her. Even in her despair, God was there as an ever present help. She knew that. How could she forget?

Painted on the back wall above the arched stain glass was a scripture, "Fear not, just believe."

Just believe, Lennox. You have to believe.

At the altar, she fell to her knees. Her broken heart splayed out like an avalanche before God. She held nothing back. She laid her fears, doubt, and brokenness in His hands.

"Do you trust Me?" A still, small voice whispered to her spirit like a rush of wind against blades of grass.

The purest warmth soothed her crushed heart.

God, I trust You, with Sky, with me, with everything. I know You care. And I know You can do anything.

When she opened her eyes, the sun broke through the clouds, lighting up the stain glass with flickering light. Red, blue, and yellow floated on the walls. Hope bubbled up on the inside of her. God could bring him back. God could raise the dead. God could do anything.

Not one Sparrow shall fall without You knowing.

She searched the front pocket of her jumpsuit and pulled out the bullet that should have killed her. She clenched it in her right fist and closed her eyes, leaning her head back and breathing in deep. She still had a purpose, for breath was still in her lungs. She would have hope regardless of the odds, regardless of what everyone said.

God kept her. He delivered her out of the hands of the enemy. *Twice.* He could deliver Sky too. She had to trust in what God was doing. Not everything in life made sense. Nothing in war made sense.

She opened her eyes and studied the bullet.

No weapon formed against me or Sky shall prosper.

Through the hardship and pain, through war and peace, through impossibilities and odds that were stacked against her, she would look to the heavens where her help came from. God was her strength and shield. He was her refuge. In Him, she had peace. In Him, she could do anything. Hope and faith made her dangerous to the enemy.

Her fight wasn't over. A new battle was on the horizon. Nothing and no one would stop her. She remained a prisoner to hope and that hope would become her weapon against the enemy. Cameron was right. The Sparrow's weapons were not carnal, but mighty through God. Lennox couldn't forget that.

She squeezed the bullet tighter and stood to her feet, seeking God to go with her into her next battle. Fear fled while faith rose.

She whispered the words her mother spoke to her years ago, staring at the light that peered through a stain-glassed window. "Sometimes one has to walk through the darkness to get to the light."

253

She was ready for the fight. She prayed. *Believed.* She would not be shaken. Not now. Not ever.

God's able.

Lennox gathered herself together and walked outside the chapel. She breathed in the fresh air and swallowed hard, looking up to the heavens. A flock of tiny red sparrows flew up from the swaying grass, spreading their wings to allow the air beneath them to sweep them higher. Lennox took it as a sign. With her heart open and fist clenched, she refused to give up.

God is with me.

Whether it was for Sky's memory or his return—she would *conquer*.

Acknowledgements

I can't go a day without thanking my Savior, Jesus Christ. Without Him, I would have never finished this book. He encourages me and motivates me in my writing. And when I want to give up, He reminds me I can do all things through Him! He is my strength when I am weak.

My family and friends are my support team and I love them to pieces. Brandon, Tyler, Jadyn, Mom, Dad, Becca, Shell, Lindsey, and my church family THANK YOU. Thank you for being there for me. Thank you for supporting me and telling me how much you loved Defier. It is the kind words that you all have spoken that have brightened up my writing days when they get dark.

My amazing friend, Veronica Lynn, who meets with me, encourages me daily and promotes my writing like nobody's business, what can I say? You have been an unmovable rock of inspiration in my life. Thank you for being you!

Angie Brashear, God placed you in my life at the perfect time! You are an incredible critique partner, who challenges me to grow and work hard. I am so thankful for our connection and I can't wait to read the third book in the Legends of the Woodlands series!

Elizabeth Miller and Nadine Brandes, thank you for providing amazing editing. Elizabeth, you are a very patient and hardworking woman to have polished Sparrow like you did. Thank you for always going the extra mile!

To my amazing launch team, you guys and gals rock! Thank you for the uplifting messages and words of encouragement. I loved getting to work with you all. Thank you for getting excited with me about Sparrow and helping to spread the word.

And finally, thank YOU, readers! I have been so blessed to have found a group of Christian readers who have given the Defier Series a chance. Thank you for giving Lennox and Sky a home on your shelves and Kindles. You have blessed me beyond measure!

About the Author

Mandy Fender is a Christian who wishes to share the gospel of Jesus through her writing. She writes Christian fiction and nonfiction. 1 Corinthians 16:14 says, "Do everything in love." and her heart is to do exactly that. She lives in the great state of Texas with her family and bulldog, Ziggy Zoo.

Connect with Mandy

Facebook: Mandy Fender Author Page
Twitter: @mandyfender11
Instagram: Mandy.Fender
Goodreads: Mandy Fender
Website: mandyfender.com

Don't miss the epic conclusion of the
Defier Series:

CONQUEROR

THE FINAL BOOK

"Tomorrow is not promised, but eternity is."

– Lennox Winters, Conqueror

How will it all end?

FIND OUT SUMMER 2017

#DEFYTHEODDS